Emily Harvale lives in East ⟨ ⟩
– although she would pref⟨ ⟩
French Alps ... or Canada ... or anywhere that
has several months of snow. Emily loves
snow almost as much as she loves Christmas.
Having worked in the City (London) for
several years, Emily returned to her home
town of Hastings where she spends her days
writing ... and wondering if it will ever snow.
You can contact her via her website, Twitter,
Facebook or Instagram.
There is also a Facebook group where fans
can chat with Emily about her books, her
writing day and life in general. Details can be
found on Emily's website.

Author contacts:
www.emilyharvale.com
www.twitter.com/emilyharvale
www.facebook.com/emilyharvalewriter
www.instagram.com/emilyharvale

***

Scan the code above to see all Emily's books on
Amazon

Lily Pond Lane series
The Cottage on Lily Pond Lane –
Part One – New beginnings and Summer secrets
Part Two – Autumn leaves and Trick or treat
Christmas on Lily Pond Lane
Return to Lily Pond Lane
A Wedding on Lily Pond Lane
Secret Wishes and Summer Kisses on Lily Pond Lane

Wyntersleap series
Christmas at Wynter House – book 1
New Beginnings at Wynter House – book 2
A Wedding at Wynter House – book 3

Merriment Bay series
Coming Home to Merriment Bay – book 1
Chasing Moonbeams in Merriment Bay – book 2
Wedding Bells in Merriment Bay – book 3

Seahorse Harbour Novels
Summer at my Sister's – book 1
Christmas at Aunt Elsie's – book 2
Just for Christmas – book 3
Tasty Treats at Seahorse Bites Café – book 4
Dreams and Schemes at The Seahorse Inn – book 5

ISBN 978-1-909917-72-9

Published by Crescent Gate Publishing

Print edition published worldwide 2021
E-edition published worldwide 2021

Editor Christina Harkness

Cover design by JR and Emily Harvale

Emily Harvale

Weddings
and
Reunions
in
Seahorse Harbour

CRESCENT GATE PUBLISHING

To the wonderful members of my Readers'
Club. Thank you so much for your
friendship and support. You know it means
the world to me. Here's to lots more books,
more chat, more sharing of fun, photos,
good times and bad and to spreading lots
more love into the world. Stay safe, well and
happy. Oh, and I hope you enjoy this book.

xx

Map of Seahorse Harbour

There's an interactive map, with more details,
on my website: www.emilyharvale.com

One

'I'm still a bit worried about Diana.'

Josie fiddled with her mug of coffee, twisting it vigorously back and forth in her hands as torrents of rain lashed the windows of Seahorse Bites Café and the waves beyond thundered towards the shore.

Elsie reached out, placing her hands gently but firmly on Josie's.

'We all are, honeybee. But trying to drill through Lyn's poor table won't help anyone.' She raised her brows before giving Josie a comforting smile.

Josie flopped back against the wooden slats of her chair. 'Sorry.'

'No need to apologise. We're all a little on edge.' Elsie patted Josie's hands and glanced out of the window. 'This weather isn't helping. I can't recall the last time we saw the sun.'

'I know. It feels like November out there, not the first day of June.' Josie puffed out a lengthy sigh before finishing off the last of her coffee. 'At least it's good for Liam's business. He's sold more ceramics over the past few days than ever because tourists want to keep as warm and dry as possible but still feel like they're seeing something worthwhile. The Olde Forge is the perfect place to do that.'

'And for everyone else's,' Lyn said, bringing a fresh pot of coffee to the table and beaming at Josie. 'Sorry love. I wasn't eavesdropping. We've been rushed off our feet day in, day out. It's a good thing I've got Nathan and now Sorcha to help out or I don't know how I'd have coped. We even had to turn people away over the weekend because we couldn't fit them all in.' She shook her head as if that bothered her. Which, no doubt it did. No one liked turning away customers and the village had been packed with tourists during the Spring bank holiday weekend. 'But Liam's work sells itself. I've had several people ask me where my gorgeous seahorse came from.'

Josie followed Lyn's gaze to the sizeable ceramic seahorse Lyn's nephew, Nathan had asked Liam to make for Lyn. That, in itself, was the best advert possible for Fulbright

Ceramics. Even Liam said he felt it was one of his best pieces.

It looked as if it were made of gold and bronze and silver, but there was also a subtle kaleidoscope of purples, greens and reds running through it. It sat proud on a shelf near the counter and the till and on a sunny day it seemed to glow. On a miserable day like this, the lighting in the café made it sparkle.

It really was incredibly beautiful. Josie had asked Lyn and Nathan if they would mind if she got Liam to make one similar for her, she loved it so much. They didn't mind at all and although Josie would never say so to them, she believed the one Liam had made for her was even more beautiful.

Liam told her it was because he had put his heart and soul into hers and she joked that although that was a wonderful sentiment, he might need those back or he could drop down dead.

'I've given all of them one of those lovely new leaflets you and Orla made,' Lyn continued. 'I even keep some in my apron pocket. See?'

She tapped her free hand against the bulging pocket on the skirt of her bright yellow apron. It held her pad and pen and a handful of the double-sided, tri-fold leaflets on which a photo of Lyn's seahorse took pride of place on the front cover.

Josie, along with Liam's daughter Orla, had designed them as a surprise present for Liam. In addition to the seahorse, the cover had a photo of The Olde Forge, and one of Liam working at his potter's wheel. It was a close-up, taken by Josie, and she'd teased him about it, saying that he looked so incredibly sexy in his faded jeans and pale blue T-shirt that people would be enticed to visit Fulbright Ceramics to see him, just as much as his work.

It was one of Josie's favourite photos of him. The sunlight had beamed through the windows of The Olde Forge that day, highlighting his lustrous chocolate-brown hair with its soft, natural waves that sat around a deeply tanned and exceedingly handsome face. His firm jaw held a hint of stubble, his dark blue eyes were focused on the vase he was shaping on his wheel, and there was a delightfully sexy smile on his lips because Josie had just told him how hot he looked.

She loved the photo so much she had it framed and hung on their bedroom wall, along with several other photos of them both, some of Orla, and even more of the three of them as a family.

Liam was thrilled with his present and once he'd given his approval, they'd had several batches of the leaflets printed and placed a stack in every shop, café and tourist attraction in Seahorse Harbour, including Seahorse Harbour Holiday Park, The Seahorse Inn and Lilith Shoe's B&B,

They'd also managed to have them on display in a number of shops, cafés and other venues in nearby Easterhill and, much to Liam's surprise, the Easterhill Hotel and Spa. The hotel manager even went as far as commissioning a couple of pieces for the hotel, and one as a present for his wife.

'Aww, thanks Lyn. That's brilliant.' Josie smiled with pride, both for Liam, and the leaflets.

Liam already had a fancy brochure that he sent out to anyone who asked for information about his work, and he had a pretty spectacular website, but the tri-fold leaflets were cheap to produce and could be slipped into someone's pocket or handbag and piled on shop counters or featured in display racks with ease.

'Asher's business hasn't noticed any difference,' Lottie piped up.

She'd hardly said a word for the half hour Josie, Elsie and she had been sitting at their table in the café, but her expression indicated she'd been deep in thought all the while.

Josie grinned. 'That's probably good, Lottie. At least it is for the pets and their owners. A boom in customers at a vet's isn't really a positive thing, is it?'

'It is if they're having boosters. Or check-ups. Or...' Lottie shrugged and let her voice trail off.

Elsie gave her a hug, smiling lovingly at her only daughter.

'That's so like you to find the positive side, sweetheart.'

A length of purple hair fell loose from the long, lime green ribbon restraining the rest of Elsie's colourful locks. She stuck out her bottom lip and blew the wayward strand from her face in a gesture more suited to a teenager than the pensioner she was.

Josie grinned at her. Elsie had never acted her age. She changed her hair colour almost monthly and wore the most outlandish clothes possible for a woman in her late sixties.

Today, the lime green ribbon exactly matched the cotton shirt-dress hanging loose over a purple and lime green T-shirt and a pair of white Capri pants. Lime green, canvas slip-ons rounded off her wardrobe – all totally inappropriate for the weather. It might be pouring with rain but it was summer as far as Elsie was concerned and Josie loved her all the more for that.

Compared to Elsie, Josie and Lottie looked ordinary. Although Josie's chestnut brown hair had been bright red last summer – mainly to annoy her mum, and Lottie's was an unusual but completely natural, strawberry blonde.

Josie wore blue jeans, a turquoise T-shirt, all-weather walking boots, and a knee-length waterproof coat that was currently slung inside out over the back of her chair.

Lottie wore black trousers, a summery floral blouse, sensible black shoes, and a pale pink waterproof jacket which also hung from the back of her own chair.

Merry, Lottie's black and white, springer spaniel, sat sphinx-like beside her chair and tried to catch droplets of water dripping from the jacket, despite the fact that Lyn had deposited a bowl of water for Merry right beside their table the moment they all sat down.

'Well, I could do with some sun,' Lyn said, refilling the three coffee mugs. 'Nathan says that, meteorologically, it's the first day of summer today. Looking out there you'd think it was the first day of winter.' She shivered dramatically for effect. 'No Diana today? I hope she's not unwell. I haven't seen her for a few days. Not since... Oh good heavens! I don't know why I said that. Sorry, loves.' She gave a small cough and glanced at the rain.

'It's all right Lyn,' Elsie said. 'We know everyone's talking about it. In fact, that's what we've been talking about this morning. I love my niece dearly, but this time she's gone too far. The trouble is, none of us is quite sure what to do.'

Josie sighed. 'We all thought Di was handling it rather well. After her initial outburst, that is.'

'You mean when Lilith told us just after Easter, right here in this café...' Lyn rolled her eyes and tutted... 'that Portia and Mikkel were engaged?'

'Yeah.' Josie nodded. 'Sometimes I could cheerfully strangle that woman. Di calmed down fairly quickly and said it didn't matter. It was only an engagement. And a few days later, she and Alex started couples' counselling. Everything seemed fine.'

'Until this weekend,' Elsie said, 'when she discovered that the wedding would be in June and she went ballistic.'

Josie shook her head. 'As everyone who was in The Seahorse Inn last Friday night can testify.'

Lyn cleared her throat. 'I missed it. But Sorcha and Nathan were there. Is she okay? Physically, I mean.'

'Physically, yes.' Josie breathed out another sigh. 'It's emotionally that's debatable. I wasn't there either, and I'm still not sure why Di had gone to the pub on her own. She's never done that as far as I know. She says it was a spur of the moment decision and that she'd gone there to prove to Mikkel and to everyone that she was fine.'

'Except she clearly isn't,' Elsie said.

'Clearly,' Josie agreed. 'But she says she was. Then the shock of hearing the wedding is so soon somehow made her see red. She overheard Mikkel telling Asher and Nathan. He didn't realise Di was there.'

Lyn shook her head. 'Poor love. Although she did bring it on herself. There's no getting away from that. Still, you can't help but feel for her, can you? And it's no wonder she was upset.'

Elsie tutted. 'Tipping up one table covered with glasses and plates might be deemed a foreseeable reaction, given the situation. Tipping up two and then racing outside before anyone could stop her and smashing Mikkel's windscreen was totally unacceptable.'

Josie shifted nervously. 'I hate to say this, but who knows what Diana might've done if Portia had been in the pub. We're all thankful she was with her dad and sister for the weekend.'

9

'And that Mikkel behaved so graciously,' Elsie added. 'He could've called the police.'

Lyn nodded and leant forward, lowering her voice to just a whisper. 'Nathan said he, Asher and Mikkel all dashed after Diana and it took all three of them to stop her doing any further damage.'

'Lottie and Sorcha made everyone else stay inside,' Elsie said, 'and they called Josie and me. We were able to calm her down and take her home and by the time Alex got back from London a few hours later, it was as if nothing had happened. We had to tell him, of course. He would've heard it from someone else if we hadn't. He was far more understanding than either of us expected.'

'I've tried everything,' Josie said, slumping forward and resting her forearms on the table. 'I even called Mum and Dad and filled them in on what happened.' She puffed out a loud sigh. 'And I only call Mum as a last resort.'

'Are they coming over?' Lyn asked.

Josie shook her head. 'No. I'm not sure if I'm glad or disappointed. Mum says I'm exaggerating as usual, and Dad says he's confident I'm the best person to handle Diana. And if I can't, then Elsie probably can. I don't think they've really grasped how serious the situation is. Mum reminded me that Di sometimes had 'temper tantrums' as a child and that once she'd got it all out of her system, she was fine. Which was true. But I told her that I thought overturning tables and smashing up other people's cars was slightly more than a temper tantrum. Mum told me not to be so dramatic. She's unbelievable at times.'

'Tibby's in denial,' Elsie said, derision of her sister evident in her tone and her expression. 'Even after all that's happened, she still can't bring herself to believe her darling Diana isn't quite as 'perfect' as she thought.'

'Perhaps what happened on Friday is a good thing,' Lyn suggested. 'Maybe your Mum's right in a way. I'm not saying I agree with her and I definitely don't think you're being overly dramatic. Certainly not from what Nathan told me. But maybe Diana's been keeping it all pent up inside, and on Friday night, she let it all out. Knowing Diana, she's probably shocked by her own behaviour. Her outburst might have made her see sense, perhaps? Given her closure. Isn't that what people call it?'

'Maybe,' Josie said. 'When I tried to talk to her about Friday night on Saturday morning, she did sort of bury her head in her hands and then she made a joke of it and said she was really embarrassed and that she'd rather not discuss it. She told me she'd send

Mikkel a note, apologising and asked me to leave it at that. She has been calm and even cheerful all weekend. She's been clearing out her kitchen cupboards and she told me yesterday that she and Alex are having the kitchen redone. Not that it needs it, but I didn't tell her that. Even so, I can't help feeling worried. But perhaps you and Mum are right. And maybe, having a project will help take her mind off Mikkel and Portia.'

'Let's hope so,' Elsie said.

'Nothing like clearing out the old and starting afresh,' Lyn said. 'I'm sure that's a good sign. It is a shame about your parents not coming over though.'

'I was certain they'd come over long before now. I know that snow storm at Christmas put paid to everyone's plans, but that was almost six months ago. Since then it's been one excuse after another.'

Elsie rolled her eyes. 'I believe Tibby is trying to avoid any unpleasantness. All the while she's at home in Gibraltar she can pretend Diana's still on that pedestal, albeit balancing rather precariously. And as much as I love your dad, my brother-in-law has never really been much good at dealing with such things. I did think that Friday's event would have got them on a plane. But it seems not.'

Josie nodded. 'I don't understand them at all. It's as if they're not living in the real world. I was sure they'd both want to come over and meet Lottie in person, even if they didn't want to deal with Diana's marital problems. They said they did, once they'd recovered from the shock. Then Mum said that's not so important because they've met via videocalls and that's "just like meeting face-to-face". Her words, not mine.'

Elsie's eyes narrowed for a split second before she smiled lovingly at Lottie.

'I was disappointed my own sister couldn't make the effort to come and meet my only daughter, but as Tibby said to me, "You've kept her a secret for more than thirty years so I really don't see why we need to rush over immediately. And now she's living in Seahorse Harbour and is engaged to that vet, it's not as if she's going anywhere." I love my sister, but sometimes I don't understand her at all.' Elsie gave Lottie another hug, shaking her head as she did so. A second strand of purple hair fell loose but this time she shoved it back in place with her fingers as she grinned at Josie. 'And sometimes, honeybee, I feel the same as you do about Lilith. I could cheerfully strangle her. Except I can't, because she's thousands of miles away.'

'It doesn't bother me,' Lottie said, once again looking as if she'd been dragged from other thoughts to join in the conversation. 'I'll admit I was looking forward to meeting my aunt and uncle, but having you, and Asher, and Josie and Diana, and all my new friends here, more than made up for that. I'll meet them one day.'

'You might have to go to Gib for that,' Josie said, smiling wanly. 'But as I've told you, meeting Mum is honestly not something to look forward to. She can be a total pain, believe me. Er. Is there something up with you, Lottie? You've seemed distracted all morning. You're here, but you're not.'

Lottie shot a look at Josie and at Elsie and then at Lyn, who remained beside the table, coffee pot in hand even though the café was packed to bursting and Nathan and Sorcha rushed around like battery-boosted bunnies, taking and fulfilling customers' orders.

'No. Nothing's up. Well. Not really. It's just that...' She let out a sigh. 'This sounds awful. Especially with everything's that's going on with Diana. And I know I'm being silly but, well, Asher and I have been planning our wedding for weeks now and we were really excited.' Lottie looked around and lowered her voice. 'Then Nathan and Sorcha announced they were getting married...' She shot an apologetic look at Lyn. 'Not that we're not thrilled about that, because we are.'

'But...?' Josie coaxed as Lottie hung her head.

'But you're beginning to feel as if there's a queue building up,' Lyn said, 'and that's taking some of the shine off planning your Big Day. Especially now that Portia and Mikkel's upcoming wedding is getting so much attention.'

'Oh.' Lottie looked surprised. 'Yes. Exactly. I'm being selfish, aren't I?'

'No, love.' Lyn smiled at her. 'It's perfectly understandable.'

'You don't have a selfish bone in your body, sweetheart,' Elsie said.

'Nope,' Josie said. 'I'd feel the same if I were planning my wedding. Which I'm not. Because Liam still hasn't proposed.'

'Are you expecting him to?' Lyn asked. 'I thought you were blissfully happy as you are.'

'We are. But I want to be his wife, not just his live-in partner.'

'Have you told him that?' Lyn scrunched up her face. 'Men aren't always that bright when it comes to things like that. I mean, look at Nathan and Sorcha.' She glanced over her shoulder but both Sorcha and Nathan were now busy in the kitchen. 'He's loved her since the day they met, but would he tell her? No.'

'He did eventually,' Lottie said. 'And now it's been suggested we have a double wedding. Sorcha and Nathan, and me and Asher.'

Lyn tutted. 'Just because Sorcha and Asher are sister and brother, it doesn't make a double wedding a good idea. I've told Nathan that and I think he agrees.'

Lottie nodded. 'So do Sorcha and Asher. It's their parents who think it's a wonderful plan.'

'What, like killing two birds with one stone, you mean?' Josie shuddered dramatically. 'Isn't that a horrible expression? I wish I hadn't said it.' She pulled a face. 'Can't Asher and Sorcha simply say no to their parents?'

Lottie shrugged. 'I'm sure they will, but they want to discuss it with them in the flesh, not over the phone or anything.'

'Then there'll be three weddings this year,' Lyn said. 'You and Asher, Sorcha and Nathan, and now, Portia and Mikkel.'

'And Portia and Mikkel's is first,' Lottie said with a dramatic sigh. 'Even though technically they were the last couple to get engaged.'

'Have you heard the news?' Lilith Shoe burst into the café, bringing a flood of rain with her. She shook her umbrella, soaking the mat in the doorway before dropping it in the iron rack containing many others, and threw her coat on the one remaining hook on the coat stand.

All eyes turned to her. Even tourists who had no idea who she was.

'Good or bad?' Lyn asked, frowning at Lilith – and the mat.

'It depends on your point of view,' Lilith said, hurrying to the table where Josie and the others sat and standing so close to Lyn their shoulders almost touched. 'Good for some, but possibly bad for every other bride-to-be in Seahorse Harbour. Which reminds me, have you heard Lucy, the school teacher and that man Kev are also getting married? They met at the Christmas Meet and Mingle Jingle. Not that that matters. Oh, and I know you only met Asher at Christmas, Lottie, so don't take that the wrong way.'

Lottie looked bereft. 'Lucy and Kev? Oh great. I mean...' She forced a smile. 'That's wonderful news.'

'That's not the news,' Lilith said, tutting. 'But I don't know why everyone's in such an almighty rush to get married. Portia and Mikkel only met at Easter. It's beyond me. And you know what they say. Marry in haste, repent at leisure. Anyway. Where was I? Oh yes. Now you know I'm not one to gossip, but

Portia's hired a wedding planner. Can you believe that?'

'A wedding planner?' Lottie looked forlorn.

'Yes. One who's apparently become quite famous over the last two years. I've never heard of her, but then I don't read bridal magazines. Her name's Breanna ... Good gracious, I forget! Oh, that's not her name.' Lilith cackled and her shoulders shook but she raced on. 'It's Breanna something-or-other. Her wedding planning business is called, The Wright Wedding and she and her team are going to be staying at the Easterhill Hotel and Spa.'

'She's got a team?' Lottie's voice was getting higher. 'How big is this wedding going to be?'

'Big, clearly,' Josie replied. 'Although this Breanna, whoever she is, will need a team if she's going to get this done by the end of the month.'

'Well,' Lilith continued, ignoring Josie and Lottie, 'I told Portia I didn't have as much as a shoebox of room. Not that she asked me, but then I suppose Mikkel told her the Sunrise B&B is always fully booked this time of year.'

'I'm surprised Portia didn't suggest they stay at Mikkel's,' Elsie said. 'His house is big enough to accommodate a "team", unless it's more than six people.'

'Perhaps Portia and Mikkel want to retain their privacy,' Josie suggested.

Lottie sighed. 'I'd like a wedding planner.'

'Would you?' Elsie seemed surprised. 'You can have one, if you want one. I'm happy to pay for that.'

Josie tutted. 'You don't need a wedding planner. You've got me and Elsie and Di. Although Diana's probably not going to be much help right now.'

'Oh yes!' Lilith boomed out excitedly. 'I heard all about Diana's little outburst at The Seahorse Inn.' She reigned back her smile with apparent difficulty. 'But as you know, I'm not one to gossip.'

Josie raised her brows. 'Since when?'

Lilith ignored her, lowering her voice a fraction, but it remained loud enough for everyone in the café to hear.

'As I was saying, my friend Doreen at the local paper, told me newsrooms across several counties are abuzz. She said Portia and Mikkel's wedding will be in magazines, and probably other newspapers too, not just the local one. After all, it's not every day that someone as rich and well-known as Portia Trulove gets married, is it? And to a man who owns the village pub, no less. Every other

19

wedding this year is going to pale in comparison. I almost feel sorry for the other brides. And that includes you, Lottie. Oh, and Sorcha too. And Lucy now, I suppose. But no one gives a fig about Lucy, do they? Although you might, Josie. Given the way she felt about Liam. All water under the bridge now though. Oh dear. I've just realised, everyone's getting married except for you and Liam! How do you feel about that?'

Two

'I still don't see why it has to be such a rush,' Tommy Trulove told his daughter, Portia for the umpteenth time since she'd arrived home for a long weekend. 'You only announced your engagement a matter of weeks ago.' But he said it with a broad smile and a twinkle in his eyes.

Portia laughed. 'Because I adore Mikkel more than I thought possible and I want to be his wife without delay. I know it might sound silly and I really can't explain it, but that's truly how I feel.'

Tommy cleared his throat and placed an arm around her shoulders, his tone a little more serious for a moment but still tinged with humour. 'You're not worried he might change his mind and go back to that married woman he'd been seeing, are you?'

'No!' Portia nudged him in the ribs and laughed again but she saw the slight hint of concern in his eyes.

Perhaps she shouldn't have told her dad about Mikkel's affair with Diana Dunn. But she had never kept secrets from him before and she wasn't going to start simply because the truth might be awkward to share.

Besides, back in April, when she'd recounted to her dad and her younger sister, Bethany, every detail of Mikkel's surprise proposal, the story about Diana had sort of tumbled out. Once she'd started, she'd had to continue.

They'd been concerned, naturally. But she'd assured them, just as Mikkel had assured her, that it was well and truly over. And she had no doubts on that score.

Although she wasn't going to tell her dad and sister about Diana's outburst in The Seahorse Inn on Friday night. Partly because she hadn't been there so she didn't know exactly what had happened and partly because all Mikkel would say about it was that there was "a bit of a scene" when Diana accidentally overheard him telling Nathan and Asher that he and Portia had decided not to wait, and were now getting married in June.

Portia had been almost as surprised as Diana obviously was when Mikkel had suggested it. But why wait? She wanted to be his wife as soon as possible, so they'd checked available dates with Perse, the vicar of St Mary Star of the Sea, the bijou Norman church in Seahorse Harbour, and they had booked the last Saturday in June, which was the next available date. And only four weeks away.

Portia wanted to tell her dad and Bethany about the wedding date face-to-face and had gone home to spend the long weekend with them.

At Bethany's request, she had decided to stay a few more days so that she, her best friend, Angela, and Bethany could go shopping for a bridal gown and bridesmaids' dresses, in spite of the fact that she was missing Mikkel dreadfully.

Soon she would be spending every day and every night with him. A few days now with her dad, her sister, and her best friend before she became a wife, somehow didn't seem too much of a sacrifice, especially as she loved them all as much as she loved Mikkel – although in different ways, of course.

'That affair was over before I came on the scene and there's no way he'll go back. He does feel guilty though, despite the fact he has no reason to. She was the one who couldn't make up her mind. Now she's behaving as if ... well, that doesn't matter. What matters is I want to start my life as Mrs Portia Meloy as soon as humanly possible.'

Tommy chuckled. 'And my eldest daughter always gets what she sets her heart on. Spend as much money as you like, my darling. I want you to have the day of your dreams. I don't think I've met this Bree Swann, have I? Are you sure she can deliver what you want?'

Bree Swann was a wedding planner with her own business which was called The Wright Wedding. Portia had met her when Bree was planning a wedding at the prestigious, Trulove Hotel in London; one of several luxury hotels in the Trulove Hotel empire. Portia happened to be visiting their London hotel that weekend and she popped into the Ballroom to see how things were going because the wedding being planned was for one of the Trulove's regular guests.

The moment she met Bree, she liked her, and they'd chatted for almost an hour. Portia had asked about the business name and Bree had explained that Wright had been her maiden name and although she was now married, both she and her husband had agreed to keep that name for the business.

Portia had taken Bree's contact details and business card with the intention of adding Bree and The Wright Wedding to a list she kept of people and businesses she was happy to recommend.

Not for one second did she think that she would be contacting Bree and asking for The Wright Wedding to plan her own Big Day.

'I'm positive. She planned the Tuffet wedding last year, at our London hotel. It was a massive success. We even got to see our hotel on the front page of several bridal magazines, remember? And without us paying a penny.'

'The Tuffet wedding? Really?' Tommy seemed surprised. 'Of course I remember that. That was her?'

'It was. Although she didn't arrange the media coverage. That came because Tiberius Tuffet, playboy billionaire, was finally getting married. But she handled it all brilliantly.'

Tommy frowned. 'There'll be media attention at your wedding, you know that, don't you? What am I saying? Of course you know. Is Mikkel prepared for that? And they're bound to dig up some dirt. That means his former affair will probably be splashed all over certain newspapers and the internet. Is the other woman aware that'll happen? And will everyone be discreet? The last thing you need as you're planning your wedding is a distraught ex-lover causing a scene, or some local gossip spreading lies and tittle-tattle.'

Hopefully, Diana wouldn't be a massive problem, but Lilith Shoe sprung into Portia's mind.

'Er. I hadn't thought about the media. I've been so excited that I didn't think about anything other than being Mrs Meloy. I'll mention it to Josie. She's Diana's twin sister. And to Elsie. She's Josie and Diana's aunt. She'll know what to do if Josie doesn't. Diana and I were sort of becoming friends until she discovered I was seeing Mikkel. Now I wouldn't be surprised if she took out a contract on me.'

'Are you serious? Do you need protection? I'll get my people on that right away.'

Portia laughed, but not altogether convincingly.

'I was joking, Dad. At least I think I was. Although Diana's husband's former lover did try to kill Diana, and hit the husband Alex instead when he dived in front to protect Diana, so maybe that's not so far-fetched. And I think someone said the woman did kill his mum.'

'What!' Tommy's face turned beetroot and his eyes almost burst out of his head as he boomed out, 'Is that true?'

'Calm down, Dad! You'll have a heart attack. I shouldn't have mentioned it. But yes. Apparently, it's true.'

'Yikes,' Bethany said, chortling as she finally looked up from scrolling on her iPad. 'It sounds like Seahorse Harbour is the set of a soap opera. I can't wait to see this place.'

Portia glanced at her. 'It does, doesn't it? I'm sure I'm safe though. Diana's upset. And she's hurting right now. But she's not the sort of woman who would take things to such extremes. I'm confident of that. There's no need to call out the dogs, Dad.'

She laughed again, this time more convincingly. The last thing she needed was her dad's security team turning up in Seahorse Harbour. Lilith Shoe would have a field day. The woman would, no doubt, try to have everyone believing the Truloves were really some sort of organised crime family, hiding behind their international hotel empire, laundering money along with their hotel bed linen.

As for Diana, she might have caused a scene of some sort at Mikkel's pub on Friday but Portia was sure the woman wasn't dangerous.

'You'll let me know if anything changes, won't you?'

'Absolutely. But it won't. Diana's nice. Not as nice as her sister, but perfectly amicable. At least she will be once she gets over Mikkel.'

'Hmm. I'll have my men on standby. Just in case.'

'Oh, Dad. You worry far too much about me. I'm a big girl. I can handle myself.'

'I don't worry about you enough. I'm serious, Portia. A woman scorned can be a dangerous thing. You've just told me as much with that tale about the husband. Keep an eye on this, Diana. Or better yet, I will.'

'I'm more concerned about Lilith Shoe.'

'Lilith Shoe?' Bethany laughed. 'What a strange name. Is she for real? Who is she? Not another of Mikkel's exes?'

A roar of laughter escaped her as Portia pictured Lilith and Mikkel together.

'No, Bethany. Lilith's the local gossip. Just like Dad mentioned. And she's really good at it. In the worst way possible. She owns the Sunrise B&B and what that woman doesn't know, isn't worth knowing about. If a pin drops somewhere in the village, Lilith Shoe will know when, where, why and who dropped it. And if she doesn't, she'll make it up.

Tommy tutted and shook his head. 'Then I'd better have someone keep an eye on her as well.'

Three

Bree was getting cross. Not enough to shout and scream, or get up and storm out of Little Pond Farm where she and her two best friends, together with their husbands, sat around Mia and Jet's massive dining table, but mad enough to scowl at her husband Garrick beneath her soot-black fringe, even though she adored him.

'Are you saying you don't want me to do this wedding?'

'That's not exactly what I meant, my darling.' Garrick reached out his hand but Bree tucked hers into her lap.

'But that *is* exactly what you said,' his twin sister, Ella pointed out, before he had a chance to continue.

'Best keep out of this,' Ella's husband, Gill suggested, pushing his glasses back in place as they inched down his aquiline nose.

Ella grinned at him and pulled a face, her mop of blonde curls dancing around her shoulders. 'No chance.'

Bree tutted. 'Portia Trulove is one of the wealthiest young women I've ever met. And she's lovely too. Not just in looks but in personality. She's virtually a celebrity. In fact, I think she is. Not that that means anything to any of you men, I realise that, but it means a great deal to me and my business. The mere fact that she wants The Wright Wedding to organise her 'Big Day' is a triumph for me. It's almost as good as getting the Queen's seal of approval. Clients will come flocking.'

'Clients are flocking now,' Mia's husband, Jet said, with just a hint of a smile on his handsome, weather-tanned face. 'I thought that was the problem. Or am I missing something?'

Mia glared at him for a second but a smile hovered on her lips. 'Are you trying to be difficult too?'

Jet's startlingly blue eyes twinkled in the candlelight. 'Me? Difficult?' He winked at his wife as the glow from the fire made his black hair sheen.

Bree tutted loudly but she couldn't be mad at Jet. Her own husband, however, was a different kettle of fish. She glared at Garrick once again and he gave a little cough.

'All I'm saying, darling, is that part of me doesn't want you to do it. The part of me that worries about you overdoing things. You're seven months' pregnant.'

'I think she's well aware of that,' Ella said, gently stroking her own bulging tummy. 'Believe me, brother dear, we women know far better than you men what we can and can't do when we're pregnant.'

'And it's not as if this is Bree's first,' Mia said. 'Unlike Ella and me.' She patted her own huge tummy which was so large now that she had to sit back from the table.

'And your point is?' Jet said, taking one of Mia's hands in his and kissing it.

'My point is, Bree knows what she's capable of. Just like Ella said. And if she thinks she can cope, then she can.'

'You seem to be forgetting one thing,' Garrick said, his tone even more serious. 'The first pregnancy was a miracle. Even more so because we had twins. We didn't expect Bree would ever fall pregnant again. But she has.'

'I *am* here, you know.'

Bree couldn't really argue with that though. After being told in her twenties that there was something wrong with her ovaries and she stood more chance of winning the lottery than she did of having a baby, both she and Garrick were astonished when they realised she was expecting.

When they discovered she was going to have twins, it was like a double miracle. Neither of them anticipated it happening again. But this time it was just one baby.

As much as she and Garrick wanted a large family, the twins were only fifteen months old, and they already had gorgeous little Flora who was almost two and a half. She was Garrick's daughter from his relationship with his former girlfriend who had died in a tragic accident, but Bree loved Flora just as much as she loved the twins. All the same, the prospect of having more than four very young children running around was daunting, so she was thankful that on this occasion, it was only one.

'I'm not trying to upset you, darling.' Garrick reached out for Bree again and this time she slipped her hand in his. 'But the doctor did say you need to take things easy.'

'I know. And I realise you're just concerned for me. But I am being careful and I promise I'm not overdoing things. Which is why my team is so busy and can't possibly manage Portia's wedding. Especially as it's only a matter of weeks until the wedding day. That's why I have to do it. It's either me, or I have to say no to Portia Trulove – my biggest and best client to date.'

'Thanks very much,' Mia said, laughing. 'I thought I was your biggest and best client.'

'You're certainly the biggest right now,' Jet said, laughing as he stood up.

He kissed her on the forehead as he went to the door to let out Little M, their dog. She'd been curled up by the fire but now clearly wanted to get to her food or water bowls, or maybe use the dog flap to go outside for a pee, in spite of the rain lashing against the windows and the wind howling through the trees and hedges and whistling around the barns in the farmyard.

'And whose fault is that?' Mia said, slapping him on the bum as he walked away from her.

'Don't blame me,' he said, grinning at her over his shoulder. 'I think it's that fortune-teller's fault.'

'Jezebella?' Bree queried.

'Yeah,' Ella said. 'We were talking about her before you and Garrick got here tonight.'

'Why?' Bree asked.

'Because this evening is to celebrate our wedding anniversary,' Mia said. 'Albeit it exactly one week late. I still can't believe we've been married for two years. It only seems like yesterday when Jet and I met. Anyway, we were reminiscing about how much has happened since Ella, Garrick and I first came to Little Pondale and the cottage in Lily Pond Lane. Naturally, we raised a toast to great aunt Mattie, even though Ella and I had to drink homemade lemonade, not wine. And then Ella mentioned Jezebella and how everything she had said has come true. Every single thing. I just wish, when she'd told me I'd get what I wanted in abundance, and that the thing with babies is that you wait for them for ages and then they all come along, one after another, she'd made it clear that three of them would come along at once. I mean, if she'd told me Jet and I would have triplets, first time around, we might not have had so much sex.'

'Then thank God she didn't!' Jet roared with laughter as he returned to the table.

'You might not be saying that when you're changing three nappies at some God forsaken hour of the morning,' Mia said, blowing him a kiss. 'And you will be the one changing them because after giving birth to three babies, I'll need lots and lots of rest.'

'I'm happy to change nappies. Although I may rope in your mum and Franklin to help. Especially as Lori did say that she and Franklin were taking the opportunity to go back to Texas for a holiday now as they won't have any free time once our babies are born.'

'Hettie and Fred have offered to help us,' Ella added, pulling a face. 'That woman should be taking it easy at her age. She must be at least ninety, but she's still running around like a teenager. Even more so after her knee replacement. At least we know she's a fantastic babysitter because she looks after Cathy's daughter often enough. And Christy's too. Although they're not babies, being eight and six, but Hettie's brilliant with them and so is Fred.'

'Yes. She's said they'll babysit for me and Jet, too. But she's not ninety, Ella, and you know that.'

Ella shrugged and grinned.

'They also babysit for us sometimes,' Bree said, feeling calmer. 'And dealing with our three little ones takes some doing. But we can both vouch for them.

'And we'll all help each other, as we do now,' Gill said.

Everyone nodded and Mia sat bolt upright. Well, as much as her huge tummy would allow.

'That's it! I've got a solution to Bree's problem.'

'You have?' Bree asked, hopefully.

'Please don't suggest Hettie and Fred should help Bree to plan this wedding,' Jet said, laughing.

'Of course not. That would be silly. Hettie and Fred haven't helped Bree in her business before. But Ella and I have. We could help with this wedding.'

'We could?' Ella didn't seem thrilled.

'Er. Hold on a minute, darling,' Jet said. 'You're eight months pregnant. With triplets.'

Mia stuck out her tongue. 'Am I? And there was me thinking I'd just put on a bit of weight. Why does that make a difference? The doctor didn't tell me to take things easy. In fact, he said he'd never known any other woman expecting triplets to be so fit and healthy and completely problem-free. No cause for concern at all. He even said I might just be a medical miracle. No morning sickness. No swollen ankles. No cravings. Well, maybe just one or two at times. My point is, Bree's the only one out of the three of us who has been told she needs to rest more. She can do that if Ella and I help out.'

'That's true,' Bree said. 'And you both know how my business runs.'

'Plus, Jet and I are silent partners, so we sort of have a duty to help, don't we?'

'I think you might have misunderstood the word "silent", oh love of my life,' Jet said, but he was grinning.

'The word isn't in my vocabulary.'

'You are forgetting one other thing the doctor said though,' Jet was more serious now. 'Triplets are usually born early. Sometimes at thirty-three weeks. You're in week thirty-three, my love. I know when we visited the doctor two days ago he said everything was fine and there was no need to do anything right now, but he'd already told us that most mothers of triplets require a caesarean section.'

'Yes. And we've discussed that option and agreed I want to see if I can give birth naturally. You worry far too much. And besides, Bree, didn't you say there's a really posh hotel nearby and that Portia said she'll pay for you and your team to stay there?'

'Yes. Easterhill Hotel and Spa.'

'You see. And I'll be in good hands with Bree and Ella.'

'You're going to be staying in a hotel?' Jet didn't look happy. 'I'm not sure I like the idea of that.'

'I promise you, the moment I feel even the slightest twinge, I'll be getting you to take me to the hospital.'

'Which I can't do if you're miles away.'

'But you'll be at the end of a phone. And Seahorse Harbour isn't very far. Don't worry. Everything will be fine.'

Ella brightened. 'A spa? I missed that bit. Okay. I'm in. We can plan this wedding from the spa, can't we? I wish it could be a bar and the spa but one out of two ain't bad.' She laughed and winked at her husband.

'Wait a minute,' Gill said. 'Are you saying the three of you will have to go and stay in some hotel, without us?'

'Yep,' Ella said. 'It gets better every second. I'll miss you dreadfully, of course. But as you're writing another book right now, I hardly see you anyway. This way you'll have the cottage all to yourself.'

'Hmmm. I'm with Jet on this. I'm not sure I like the sound of that.'

'But Bree needs our help,' Mia said. 'You'd all do the same if you were in our shoes.'

None of the men could argue with that.

'I still don't like it,' Jet said. 'But I know once you've made up your mind you won't change it, and I can see by your face that you have, so I won't bother to fight that battle. I don't see why you have to stay at a hotel though. Why can't I drive you there each day? And you said yourself that Seahorse Harbour's not that far from here.'

'Are you worried Mia might get chatted up?' Ella laughed. 'Have you seen the size of your wife?'

Jet grinned at that. 'Yes. And she looks even more beautiful now than she did the day I fell in love with her. That's not what worries me. What worries me is the timing, and also the same thing that is worrying Garrick, and will now be worrying Gill. All three of you are pregnant. Some more so than others. And as I said, Mia might give birth early, as most women carrying twins or triplets do. You did when you had your twins, Bree. I want to be by her side when that happens. Not miles away. I want to make sure she's okay and that I can get her to the hospital in plenty of time.'

'Oh Jet, my love.' Mia blew Jet a big kiss. 'You can be such a guy sometimes. Babies don't shoot out when the water breaks. Well, maybe some do. But my womb's not like one of those theme park water rides, you know. Even if I am miles away, I'm sure you'll have plenty of time to get me to the hospital. And I bet Easterhill has a hospital, so I'll be nearer to one there than I am here. Right. That's settled. Bree, Ella and I will go to Seahorse Harbour and plan this wedding. And it'll be our little treat before we have to go through all the pain and suffering of giving birth. That seems only fair.'

'I agree,' Ella said. 'You three men can stay here and make sure all our homes are totally ready for our new arrivals. That sounds like a brilliant plan to me.'

'Our cottage has been ready for weeks now,' Gill said, smiling slightly in spite of a small furrow of concern between his brows. 'And our baby isn't due for another three months.'

'Then this'll be like a boy's holiday for all of you, too,' said Ella. 'Enjoy it while you can. There soon won't be any peace and quiet for miles around in Little Pondale.'

Garrick finally laughed. 'Welcome to our world. Our cottage hasn't had a day of peace and quiet ever since the twins were born. Flora was a saint compared to them. Now she seems to want to compete to see who can make the most noise.'

'That's true,' Bree said. 'But it's been wonderful. Truly wonderful.'

Garrick kissed Bree on the lips. 'It has, my darling. And I wouldn't change a thing.' He gently brushed a wayward strand of her hair away from her eyes with his fingertips. 'I suppose you'd better call this Portia woman back and tell her to book the hotel for you and your team of trusty aides. And I'll look after the kids with my team of trusty aides. And that means you and Gill, Jet. Not just Hettie and Fred.'

'That part's fine with me,' Jet said. 'Gill and I need all the hands-on experience we can get. But I still don't see why you all have to stay at some hotel.'

'It'll only be for a week at most,' Bree replied. 'And then for the weekend of the wedding to make sure it all goes to plan. Once I've got things up and running, I can coordinate everything from here. Although I might have to nip back every now and then if Portia needs me, but Mia and Ella probably won't have to join me for that.'

Jet stared directly at Mia and took her hands in his.

'And what happens when I need you, Mia? You do realise that this will be the first time we'll be apart since you moved in here, don't you? I'm not sure how I feel about that. And you must promise me, the moment you feel anything might be happening, even if it's a false alarm, you'll call me right away, no matter what time it is, okay? But I'm still not entirely happy about this. And the sooner you're back home, safe and sound, the more relieved I'll be.'

'Oh, Jet, my darling. We're going to Seahorse Harbour, not the Outer Hebrides. Everything will be fine. Just you wait and see.'

Four

Diana paced the tiled kitchen floor of Sea View Cottage, which contrary to its name wasn't really a cottage but a large, impressive ultra-modern house, with lots of glass instead of solid walls, all of which currently resembled some massive water feature, as torrential rain streamed down the huge panes and splashed into the swimming pool that sat to one side of the decking.

She stopped for a second or two in front of the glass doors overlooking her garden, and watched as her plants and flowers that were lit up by a number of colour changing lights the size of footballs, took a battering.

Sighing loudly, she turned and paced back towards the kettle, switching it on ... and off ... and on and off again.

'A hot tap is definitely going on my list, Henry,' she said to the family dog. 'I hate waiting for the kettle to boil. Not that I want a cup of tea. I don't know what I want.'

Henry was sprawled on the sofa in the large open plan kitchen, dining and sitting area, snoring loudly, but his head shot up at the mention of his name and a moment later, he let out a pensive bark, as if he'd given it some thought.

'You're right,' Diana said. 'I want more wine.'

Diana went to the cooler, took out a bottle of her favourite Sancerre and poured herself a very large glass, despite the fact that it was almost midnight and she was the only human in the house.

'I wonder if there's such a thing as a wine tap? What do you think about that?'

Henry tipped his head to one side and raised his upper lip in something akin to a sneer. But he often did that when he had been dozing and was only half awake. He yawned, shook his head and let it flop back onto the cushions, with a soft sort of growl.

'Okay. Don't get all righteous with me. I've had enough of that from everyone else. I don't need it from you.' She sat beside him in the space on the sofa she'd vacated minutes earlier and gently stroked the soft brown, white and tan fur on his head, avoiding his wiry brows that resembled those of an Irish Wolfhound. 'You do still love me, don't you?'

He made a sort of 'mmmmm' sound which Diana took as a yes.

'And Josie says she does too. So that's good, isn't it?'

Henry opened one eye; the one with a big autumn-red shape over it, licked his lips, and closed his eye again.

'I assume that means you agree. But Mikkel definitely doesn't.' She chugged down half her glass of wine. 'I don't know what went wrong. If only I'd realised how I felt sooner. Not that I'm really sure how I feel anymore. I was certain I'd love Alex for the rest of my life. And I still do, so I don't understand what's changed. But I realised I love Mikkel too. Even more than I love Alex.'

Henry didn't respond so she emptied her wine glass and got up for a refill, at which point he lifted his head again and watched her until she returned to her spot beside him.

'Don't worry. I'm coming back. Did you think I might go rushing off to see Mikkel? You heard me promise Josie when she was here tonight that I wouldn't, so as much as I want to, I won't. She'd kill me if she found out. And she would, you know. Someone in this bloody village would tell her. And that cow Lilith probably has a video camera aimed at Mikkel's drive so that she can see who comes and goes. Not that I'm sure she can see Mikkel's drive from the Sunrise B&B.

But she'd find out I was there and announce it to everyone. You can bet on that.'

She dropped onto the sofa and reached out for Henry again. He shifted his position slightly so that his long legs, which made him look like a Great Dane when standing, draped across Diana. His tail, which was similar to a Golden Retriever's and could clear a coffee table in seconds with just one wag, thumped against the sofa cushions. He might be a mongrel, and at times was very naughty, but he was gorgeous. Diana, who usually preferred things to be 'perfect' loved him to bits, as did everyone who met him.

'Perhaps I should've gone back to our house in Blackheath with Alex. But what's the point? He'd be working at the hospital all hours and the kids are at school so I'd be completely on my own there. Apart from you. At least staying here, I have Josie and Elsie and Lottie and Sorcha and, well, everyone else. And you. I love you, Henry.'

She snuggled up against him and tried to remind herself just how lucky she was – which was something that Josie had pointed out more than once that evening.

'You've got more than most women could dream of having,' Josie had said. 'And in spite of how I felt about Alex and his behaviour, he's definitely changed and he clearly adores you. You've always told me that Alex was the love of your life and that you'd never love anyone as much as you love him. I don't know why that's suddenly changed, but don't throw it all away because you now think you're in love with another man. Especially as that man has made it clear that you and he will never have a future together now.'

'Thanks for rubbing that in,' Diana had snapped.

But Josie was right. Diana had said those things. That was why, soon after the first time she left Alex, which was only last summer, she'd ended her affair with Mikkel and taken Alex back.

And Alex had definitely changed. Josie was right about that. Especially after his brush with death at Christmas. His wandering eye seemed to have stopped wandering and he'd fixed his gaze and all his love and attention, firmly on his wife.

At the time, Diana had been thrilled and hopeful for the future, but at Lottie and Asher's engagement party in February, something had changed within her.

She wondered how long the 'new' Alex would last. She questioned her feelings for him. She considered her future and what she really wanted from it.

The kids were growing fast. Becca was sixteen now but would be seventeen in a few months. She was already in a strong and loving relationship with her boyfriend, Noah and she'd be going off to uni next year – although she and Noah had been talking of travelling for a year once he'd left uni, so Becca might delay her education to do that.

The 'old' Diana and Alex would've tried to put a stop to that. The 'new' Diana and Alex now only wanted what was best for their kids and if that meant Becca and Noah backpacking around the world, then so be it. Even though Diana would be worried sick about her daughter. Noah had a good head on his shoulders and he absolutely adored Becca, so he would take excellent care of her, Diana was certain of that.

Toby was fourteen, coming up for fifteen, and like Becca, was currently at boarding school, although both were only weekly boarders and came home every weekend. Unless school events, or stays with friends prevented that. Toby had already said he wanted to go away with his friends in the Air Cadets this summer. That was something Alex had got Toby involved with. Alex loved flying and had a light aircraft at the Easterhill air club and he'd started taking Toby with him more and more.

Until then, Toby had spent most of his time with his nose virtually glued to his phone, apart from when he was on the beach surfing, boarding or sailing with Asher and Liam and Mikkel, or training to be a junior Seahorse Rider. Asher, Liam and Mikkel were all Seahorse Riders and they treated Toby as a friend, rather than the kid he was.

The Seahorse Riders were volunteers who looked after the local population of seahorses that lived in an area of the coastline in Seahorse Harbour called The Shallows. This was an inlet at the foot of Seahorse Cliffs and was nestled between the cliffs and Seahorse Point. From the air, the entire coastline forming Seahorse Harbour and its surrounds, looked like a seahorse. Seahorse Point was situated at the tip of what would've been a seahorse's snout and The Shallows could be found beneath what was effectively a seahorse's chin.

Not that Diana was sure that a seahorse had a chin. In all the years she had visited, and then lived in, Seahorse Harbour, she knew little about the tiny creatures themselves. Both Mikkel and Toby had tried to educate her on the subject but in all honesty, she had never been that interested in what lived in the sea. She wasn't a huge fan of the sea water either; by far preferring to swim in her pristine and crystal-clear pool.

Would Toby's relationship with Mikkel change because of her recent behaviour?

Diana cringed at the thought.

Why had she behaved like some mad woman on Friday night? Why couldn't she just accept that Mikkel no longer loved her? Why couldn't she simply be grateful and thankful for what she had?

And she had a lot. Josie was right about that too.

She glanced around her. Sea View Cottage was wonderful. There were views of the sea to be had from three sides; the front, the back and one side, although on a day like this you couldn't see much of the sea and tonight, the lights of passing ships were completely obscured by the torrential rain.

The cottage had an impressive pool that, thanks to its position, got the sun for most of the day. When there was sun, that is. It was surrounded by a spacious wooden deck where she and Josie had lounged most of last summer and would no doubt do the same this summer. If the weather ever improved.

Upstairs, the cottage had several bedrooms with en suites, and downstairs, the large hall had a cloakroom and Alex's study to one side, two steps down into the open plan kitchen, and a rather grand staircase to the floor above.

The kitchen itself was huge by most standards with a cavernous dining area to the left that led into a rather grandiose sitting room, although one section of the kitchen also had a spacious but cosy, sitting area overlooking the garden and that was where she and Henry were sitting right now.

The kitchen also had two sets of folding doors, one straight ahead that overlooked the garden and a gate that led from there out into Little Wood, which was a large and public area of woodland. The other set of doors opened onto the spacious decked area which surrounded two sides of the house. That, in turn, led to an immaculate lawn edged by more gorgeous, plants, shrubs and trees. All of which were currently being pummelled by the rain.

But it wasn't just the material things in her life she should be thankful for, or her now doting, husband and her wonderful kids.

She also had a twin sister who had, and would continue to, stand by her through thick and thin. An incredible if somewhat oddball aunt, who would do the same. And only last Christmas she and Josie had discovered that Elsie had a daughter – their cousin, Lottie, who had quickly become not just a relative but a great friend.

And she had other friends in Seahorse Harbour. Liam and Asher ... and Mikkel.

Was he still her friend?

He could've called the police on Friday but he didn't.

He even told her he understood and that he'd already forgiven her.

But he did warn her not to do anything like it again, and to stay away from Portia if she felt any ill will towards his fiancée.

His fiancée.

How the hell had that happened?

And now he was marrying the bloody woman.

This month, in fact.

She hoped it would rain on that day.

And she hated herself for wishing that.

'Am I going mad, Henry? Is that what's happening to me? Is that what happened to Marina before she tried to run me down at Christmas and hit Alex instead? Is this what Love does to people who fall for someone they can't have?' She sipped her wine, slowly and thoughtfully now. 'Alex must truly love me, mustn't he, to have leapt in front of that car and risked his life to save mine? And I do still love him. So why do I want Mikkel so badly? And why does this hurt so much? Oh, Henry, what am I going to do?'

Henry opened his mouth as if he were about to give her an answer, just as her phone pinged with a text.

'Hold that thought, Henry. This might be Mikkel!'

She sat upright and so did Henry and he gave a quick bark as she grabbed the phone from the side table.

But it wasn't a text from Mikkel. It was from Alex.

'You asleep?' it read.

'Yes,' she replied. But she added a smiley emoji.

A second or so later the phone rang and a photo of Alex's handsome face popped up on the screen.

'Who's this?' she asked, smiling in spite of her misery.

'A man who loves you. Very much, in fact. And who wants you to know he's been thinking about you all day and all evening. Sorry it's so late but we had a couple of emergencies and you know how short-staffed we are. How are you? Did Josie come round? Is she staying again tonight?'

Alex had returned to their Blackheath home first thing on Monday morning. As one of the youngest and most sought-after heart surgeons at his London hospital, Diana wouldn't let him call in sick, or take a sudden holiday to spend time with his 'emotionally unstable' wife. Her words, not his.

Even so, he had wanted to, but Josie had offered to spend all day Monday and all Monday night with Diana – and had done so – so he had gone to work.

Josie also offered to spend Tuesday with Diana, but Diana wanted to have some time alone to think. And to sleep. She was tired and drained and emotionally wrung out.

Alex had phoned three times during the day, and Josie popped round in the evening, with pizza and a bottle of wine, so the wine Diana was currently drinking was her second bottle of the day.

Not that she cared.

Except for the fact that she couldn't sleep.

'Josie came with pizza and wine, and she did offer to stay again, but I want to be on my own.'

'Are you sure that's wise? Sometimes it's better to have company when we're not feeling like our usual selves.'

'Is that a polite way of saying that Josie should be here in case I go nuts again? Don't worry, Alex. Been there, done that, still wearing the T-shirt.'

'That wasn't what I meant. I simply thought it might be nice to have someone to talk to.'

'I've been chatting with Henry. He's quite talkative you know.'

'Henry? You mean our dog?'

'Now you're saying I'm crazy because I'm having a conversation with our dog?'

'Absolutely not!' He laughed but the nervousness came across loud and clear. 'I often chat with Henry. But he thinks he's smarter than me.'

'He's definitely smarter than me.' She smiled at Henry, grateful that Alex had at least tried to make a joke of it.

'But he's not as gorgeous as you. Listen. Tomorrow's jammed, so I can't get away until Thursday but I'm going to try to finish early by switching some of the more mundane procedures with a colleague. Why don't I drive down and take you somewhere special? What about dinner at the Easterhill Hotel? Better yet. Why don't you and Josie, and Elsie and Lottie if they want to, book yourselves some treatments during the day. I'll pay. And for a cab there and back for them. I'll book a room for us, and you and I can have dinner and spend the night. Is that a date? I've got to come back on Friday for a couple of ops, but I'll collect the kids from their schools, and we'll all return for the weekend. How does that sound? Unless you'd rather come up here and I'll book The Savoy or somewhere?'

He was trying so hard and she had to give him credit for that. She was surprised he'd forgiven her so easily. But then again, she'd forgiven him all his affairs time and time again. At least she'd only had the one.

Well, strictly speaking two – but with the same man, twice, so that only counted as one, didn't it? And she hadn't slept with Mikkel since the day she'd taken Alex back last year. Although not for want of trying. It was Mikkel who wouldn't play ball.

'Dinner and a night at the hotel sound great. But I'll have to ask Josie or Elsie to look after Henry. And I'd prefer the Easterhill Hotel if that's okay. I don't feel up to travelling far.'

'The Easterhill it is then.'

'Thanks, Alex. I'll ask Josie in the morning.'

'Excellent. I'm sure either she or Elsie will happily take care of Henry. I'll see you at the hotel on Thursday. Now try to get some sleep. I love you, Diana. More than you can imagine.'

'I love you too.'

And she did.

But not as much as she now loved Mikkel.

And that was a serious problem.

Five

The Easterhill Hotel and Spa was exactly as Bree had imagined. Not that she had needed to imagine it. The first thing Ella had done, as they'd all sat around the dining table at Mia and Jet's, once they'd agreed that she and Mia would help out Bree, was look up the hotel on the internet.

Bree had been over the moon when she'd seen the plush rooms and comfy-looking beds. Ella had cooed like a mother hen over the swimming pool, the spacious spa and well-equipped gym.

That had made Gill laugh.

'Have you ever been to a gym?'

'I've looked at them,' Ella said.

'You don't have to go into one to appreciate how great they are,' Mia said. 'But let's move on. What's the restaurant like and is there only one? And where's the menu?'

Ella gave her a gentle prod in the tummy. 'Don't you think you should avoid the restaurant? You can't get much more in this tummy of yours, can you?'

'I'm eating for four, don't forget. And these babies have got Jet's insatiable appetite.'

Jet roared with laughter. 'I thought I'd be to blame, somehow, my love. But my insatiable appetite is for you, not for food.' He pulled her close. 'How long are you going to be away? I'm missing you already.'

They shared a passionate kiss and Ella made a choking sound.

'Get a room, will you?'

Jet eased himself away from Mia and threw Ella a mischievous grin.

'I just might. At the Easterhill Hotel and Spa.'

He was joking, of course, but Bree wouldn't be at all surprised if he did turn up. He adored Mia and despite his humour, everyone could see he wasn't entirely happy with the thought of being separated from her.

Bree hadn't known him before he and Mia got together but she'd heard the stories from others in the village of Little Pondale where Jet had lived his entire life.

They'd all said how wild he was as a boy, and how, the minute he was old enough to date, he'd broken the heart of every woman who fell for his abundant charms. But he'd been honest with each one. He wasn't looking for love, or for a relationship and definitely not for a wife.

Until he met Mia and she turned his world upside down.

Ella had told Bree that Jet had fought his feelings for Mia at first, irrationally believing that he was "just like his dad" and would ultimately let her down and break her heart, which was something he wasn't prepared to do because secretly, he loved her. So instead, he'd kept her at arms' length and pretended all he felt for her was friendship.

But Mia wasn't having that, and eventually Jet had admitted how he felt. He had fallen so deeply in love with her that he couldn't bear the thought of life without her by his side.

Prior to Mia, no woman had ever been able to entice him into a relationship, let alone anything more.

Since meeting her, he was the poster-boy for Love – the picture of happiness, and was now eagerly looking forward to being a father. And he'd vowed that he would never be anything like his own father had been.

'If you really aren't happy about this, Jet,' Mia had said, 'then I won't go. I know you don't want to be away from me for even one day, let alone one week, and I feel the same. But it is only one week out of all the weeks we've had together and all the weeks we will have together in the future. Remember, Jezebella told me I'd lead a long and blissfully happy life with the man I loved, and she's been right about everything so far.'

'I know. I realise I'm being foolish and unreasonable and behaving like a bit of a nutter. And you're right. One week is nothing in the scheme of things. It just feels like a lifetime right now. Don't worry about me though. It'll be fine. And by the time you come home, both Gill and I will be experts at this nappy changing lark. We've already had a bit of experience, but a week without the women in our lives will make us 'superdads'. And Garrick will be a good tutor, I'm sure.'

'You're already a 'superdad',' Mia said. 'And the most wonderful, sensational husband and lover and friend. And think how great it'll be when we spend our first night together after a week apart.'

'Oh bloody Nora!' Ella said. 'Will you two stop. You're making me feel quite queasy.'

They'd all laughed at that but Bree had seen the look in Jet's incredible eyes, and in spite of his reassuring words, it was clear to her that he still wasn't entirely convinced this was a good idea.

It had made Bree feel somewhat guilty. Mia and Ella were doing this for her. But that was what friends did for one another, wasn't it? She would do the same for them and Jet would do the same for Gill or Garrick if they asked him to, so it wasn't that unreasonable.

And one week wasn't long. Bree would miss Garrick and the kids just as much as Jet and Mia, and Ella and Gill would miss each other.

For one brief moment, Bree had considered calling Portia Trulove and telling her that she would have to find herself another wedding planner. This was causing too much upheaval for too many people.

But then she remembered how The Wright Wedding had been inundated with calls and bookings after the Tuffet wedding last year and how Portia Trulove was just as well-known as Tiberius Tuffet.

This wedding would make headline news in certain sections of the media and that was worth almost any amount of upheaval, especially as everything would soon get back to normal after the wedding.

And now that she, Mia and Ella stood in the lobby of the Easterhill Hotel and Spa with all and sundry staff running around to take their bags and provide them with their every need – all at Portia's expense, Bree was rather glad she had said yes.

They'd arrived on Wednesday evening because Bree wanted to get settled in and make an early start on Thursday morning. Jet, Garrick and Gill had insisted on taking them.

Ella and Gill travelled with Mia and Jet whilst Bree travelled with Garrick, having left Hettie and Fred to look after Flora and the twins for a couple of hours.

That meant Garrick was torn between spending more time with Bree, looking around the hotel and helping her settle in, or dashing back to the children. In the end, after much reassurance from Bree, and a little encouragement from his sister Ella, he chose the children.

But at least Jet and Gill left at the same time, because the plan had been for Jet to leave the car he'd driven – which was Mia's – at the hotel, just in case the women needed one, and for Jet and Gill to return to Little Pondale with Garrick. At the end of the week, Garrick would drive the men back to the hotel, and Jet would collect Mia's car.

Nevertheless, when it came to it, Garrick, Jet and Gill had all been very reluctant to depart. If it hadn't been for the fact that neither Garrick nor Bree would consider leaving their children with others overnight, no matter how dependable those others might be, all three men would've probably stayed until the morning.

'There'll be tears,' Ella said, as she, Mia and Bree waved their husbands off. 'And most of those will be shed by Gill. He's such a softie at heart. Now let's go and look at the spa.'

Six

'It's good to see you again, Bree,' Portia said, walking towards the table on the terrace of the Easterhill Hotel and Spa, where Bree, Mia and Ella sat enjoying hearty breakfasts and soaking up some early morning sunshine.

The terrace overlooked the elaborately designed and breath-takingly beautiful gardens which had a tall, five-tiered, ornate fountain in the centre of an immaculate lawn. That, in turn, was surrounded by borders of stunningly gorgeous flowers and exotic trees, palms, ferns and a variety of long grasses swaying to and fro in the gentle, morning breeze.

'Portia! Hello. How are you?'

'I'm well, thanks. And all the better for seeing the sun after so many days of rain.'

Rain was forecast again for later, so it was good to see a bit of sun – however briefly.

Bree, Mia and Ella all rose slowly and awkwardly to their feet.

'May was one of the wettest months of the year so far,' Bree said. 'Let's hope this month isn't the same. Especially not for your wedding.'

Portia stopped and stared at the three women. 'Oh my goodness. You're all ...' She hesitated, not wishing to cause any offence.

'Pregnant?' the blonde woman said. 'Yes. Is that a problem? I'm Ella.'

'A problem?' Portia laughed. 'No, not at all. Just a surprise. Why didn't you mention it, Bree?'

'Sorry, Portia.' Bree looked embarrassed. 'I should've said. These are my two best friends and my best assistants, of course. Nothing but the best for you. Oh, this is Mia Cross. And Ella Swann – sorry. Ella De Fonteneau, I should say. I don't know why I keep calling you by your maiden name, Ella. Anyway, Ella's already introduced herself.'

Ella rolled her eyes but didn't comment.

Portia smiled at Mia and Ella. 'Hello, Mia. It's great to meet you. And you too, Ella. Er ... did you say Swann? Isn't that your married name, Bree? I know you use your maiden name for the business because you told me so, but Swann is your surname too. Or am I mistaken?'

Ella now wrapped an arm around Bree's shoulder. 'You're right. Bree's married to my twin brother. Nothing like keeping it in the family. And Mia and her husband, Jet are silent partners of The Wright Wedding. Oh. But perhaps I shouldn't be telling you that. Sorry, Bree.'

Bree smiled. 'I don't mind at all. I wouldn't have my business if it hadn't been for Mia and Jet's generosity.'

'Nonsense,' Mia said, 'You're brilliant at your job.' She beamed at Portia. 'My wedding was Bree's first event and I can tell you, it was the best day of my life. And not just because I was getting married to the man of my dreams, but also because Bree thought of everything and made it all look so easy and such fun.'

'That's good to know.' It was wonderful that these three women clearly supported each other and were obviously great friends. The fact that they were all several months pregnant didn't worry Portia. Although she hoped none of them would decide to give birth on or near her wedding day. That might cause a few headaches. 'I'm marrying the man of my dreams too, and I can't wait to be his wife. That's why you don't have much time, I'm afraid. I could delay things, but I just don't want to.'

'Bree planned Mia's wedding in about the same amount of time,' Ella said. 'And that was before Bree had any contacts in the wedding industry. Now she knows everyone who matters, so this should be a breeze. But I will admit that the three of us don't move quite as fast as we did before we fell pregnant, so don't expect to see any of us running anywhere, anytime soon.'

'I have people who can do any running required,' Portia replied. 'But please sit down. Do you mind if I join you? I was so excited this morning I left home without having breakfast.'

'Please do,' Bree said.

'We don't mind at all,' said Ella. 'Besides, you are paying for it.'

'Ella!' Mia said. 'That was rude.'

'Why? It's true.'

Portia burst out laughing. 'It's okay. I don't mind at all. And yes. I'm paying for this and anything else you want or need while you're here. Including a doctor if one proves necessary. Which I hope it won't. And it's going to be worth every penny, I'm already certain of that.'

No sooner had she sat down than a waiter hurried over.

'Would you like to see a menu, Miss Trulove?'

'No thanks. May I have some wholemeal toast, please? And coffee. Oh, and orange juice. Would you ladies like anything else?'

All three of them shook their heads and declined.

Portia smiled at the waiter who looked as if he was almost bowing.

'That's it then, thanks.'

'Does that happen often?' Ella asked. 'I thought Mia got great service – she's loaded too, you know, although she's nowhere near as rich as you – but no one bows to her.'

'He wasn't bowing, exactly, but yes. I'm ashamed to say it does.'

'There's no need to feel ashamed of that,' Ella said. 'I'd love it if people bowed to me. I keep trying to get my husband to, but he won't. And we've only been married a year, so it's all downhill from here. Soon he'll refuse to bring me coffee in bed every morning, and rub my feet every night. You just can't get the staff these days.'

'She's joking,' Mia said, grinning.

'I'm not,' Ella said, with a wink.

'Er.' Bree seemed hesitant. 'If our being pregnant does worry you, you would say so, wouldn't you? I will admit I didn't want to tell you over the phone in case it gave you pause for thought. But I promise you we'll all give our best and we won't let you down.'

Portia smiled at Bree and placed a hand reassuringly on her arm.

'It doesn't bother me one bit. I think we're all going to have a lot of fun planning this wedding. But there is one tiny thing I should mention. Well, more than one. And I hope this won't put you off.'

'Nothing will do that,' Bree said.

Portia took a deep breath. 'This isn't the only wedding taking place in Seahorse Harbour, but mine is the first. And I may have inadvertently caused a little bit of resentment because of that. Some of my fiancé's friends are also getting married this summer.'

'Are their weddings this month too?' Ella asked.

'No. Asher Bryant is marrying Lottie Short and they were talking of getting married later in the year but things have changed because now Asher's sister, Sorcha is marrying Nathan Bromley, and Asher and Sorcha's parents have suggested a double wedding for this summer. It won't be before mine because the last Saturday in June was the earliest date we could get at the village church, but it may be soon after.'

'Wow,' Ella said, laughing. 'Perhaps they could do with a wedding planner too, Bree.'

'I'm happy to introduce you,' Portia said, as the waiter returned with her toast, coffee and orange juice and placed them on the table. He was about to pour her coffee but she stopped him.

'I can do that, thanks.'

'As you wish, Miss Trulove. May I get you anything else?'

'Not right now, thanks. This looks perfect.'

'Enjoy.' This time he did give a tiny bow as he stepped away.

'Er. Thanks, Portia,' Bree said, eyeing the waiter. 'That's so kind. But I think your wedding will be the last I'll be taking on until after all our babies are born.'

'I understand. Well, anyway. All these names won't mean anything to you now but I wanted you to know about them because you'll be meeting them sooner or later. And also because they'll possibly be wanting many of the things we will. Like a wedding cake etc.'

'Okay. I'll make a note of them.' Bree typed the names into her phone as Portia poured herself some coffee. 'I keep notes on here as well as on my laptop.'

'Won't one of your hotel chefs, or bakers or whatever make your cake?' Ella asked. 'I looked up some of your hotels and you've got the best of the best. Michelin stars and the lot.'

'I did consider that, and my dad thinks I should, but how do I pick one over another? And besides, there's a brilliant baker in Seahorse Harbour. Her name's Bev and she owns and runs, Beach Bakers on Sea Walk. I'll introduce you to her later today. I've already asked her if she'd be willing to make my cake, and she is, but the sooner we book her the better. I know you probably have people you use and can highly recommend, and I wasn't sure how this all works, but I like the idea of using local people for as much as possible, especially as the village will be my future home.'

'You're moving to Seahorse Harbour?' Ella seemed surprised. 'You could live anywhere in the world, couldn't you?'

'I could. And I've chosen Seahorse Harbour. Wait until you see it. It's a magical place. Plus, my fiancé owns the only pub in the village, a restaurant, a nightclub, and a quirky rental property. Plus, we're jointly buying Seahorse Harbour Holiday Park, and replacing it with a luxury eco hotel, so neither of us would want to live anywhere else.'

'We chose to live in Little Pondale,' Mia said. 'Why are you so surprised that Portia would want to live somewhere other than Seahorse Harbour?'

Ella shrugged. 'I suppose because Portia's a celebrity. As much as I love you and as rich as you are, you're not.'

Mia laughed out loud. 'You're an idiot, Ella.'

Ella grinned. 'Tell me something I don't know.'

'We'll look forward to meeting Bev today,' Bree said, throwing Ella and Mia a slightly disapproving frown, like a mother to her naughty children. 'I do have a list of bakers I would normally use, but this is your wedding, Portia, and if you'd like to deal with local people that's perfectly okay with me.'

'Providing they're up to Bree's high standards,' Ella said, with a grin.

Portia smiled. 'I'm sure Bev will be. If she didn't have her own business in the village, I'd offer her a job at any one of our hotels, she's that good.'

'Excellent,' Bree said.

'In addition to the couples I mentioned,' Portia continued, 'another couple have decided to marry this summer. Lucy Willis, who's a school teacher here in Easterhill but lives in Seahorse Harbour is marrying her boyfriend, Kev. I don't know his surname. He doesn't live in the village but they see each other every weekend and apparently he's about to move down for good.' She laughed and shook her head. 'I have that news directly from the woman who knows everything in Seahorse Harbour – Lilith Shoe. I need to warn you about her. She spreads rumours and gossip like I spread butter on my toast.' She tapped her slice of toast and butter with her knife to emphasise her point.

'Every village has one,' Ella chirped. 'Ours is called Hettie and she's one hundred and two.'

Mia tutted. 'Poor Hettie is getting older every time you say her name.'

'We all are.' Ella grinned. 'Okay, Hettie's not that old, and she's actually really nice, once you get to know her. She's weird though. When we met her, she told us she lived with her husband, Hector, and Prince Gustav.'

'Oh. She imagined a Prince Gustav lived with them?' Portia queried.

'No. Prince Gustav did live with her. He still does. He was one of the ring-bearer's at her wedding. He's her pet, a white rat. It was her husband that was the weird bit.'

Portia shivered. 'A pet white rat seems weird to me. Why was her husband weird?'

'He was dead.'

Portia choked on the bite of toast she'd just taken and had to wash it down with a slug of coffee.

'Are you telling me she kept her dead husband in her home?'

Ella laughed hysterically and shook her blonde curls. 'Oh no. She's not that weird. Although in Little Pondale anything is possible. Don't get me started on the curse of Frog's Hollow. Or the white witch, Aurelia Jenkins and her fortune-telling sister, Jezebella. No. Hector was dead and buried. It was actually the curse of Frog's Hollow that killed him. But Hettie behaved as if he was still with her. She talked to him and everything. Until she met and married Fred Turner and Hector gave his blessing and moved on to the afterlife, or wherever she said he went.'

Portia laughed and shook her head. 'Flipping heck. And I thought Seahorse Harbour had some odd characters.'

'You were telling us about Lilith Shoe, Portia,' Bree said, giving Ella another one of her looks.

'Oh yes. The problem with Lilith is that if she can't find anything true to gossip about, she can easily make things up. And she can twist conversations so that you believe one thing when really the total opposite is true. She ... she has upset one or two people and she could've ruined my relationship with Mikkel before it really began, except I wanted to hear it from the man himself.'

'I see.' Bree added something to the notes on her phone.

Portia took a deep breath and let it out slowly, leaning forward as she did so before taking a soothing sip of her coffee.

'Which brings me to another matter. I'm not sure I should be telling you this, and it makes me sound like a gossip to do so, but I need you to be aware of someone who ... let's just say, isn't entirely thrilled about my upcoming wedding.'

All three friends leant closer.

'We won't repeat anything you tell us,' Mia assured her.

'We're good at keeping secrets,' Ella added. 'Especially Mia. Her great aunt Mattie was a spy, you know.'

'A spy? Really?' Portia was impressed.

Bree glared at Ella. 'Which has nothing whatsoever to do with this wedding or what Portia was about to tell us.'

'I didn't say it did.'

'I'd like to hear more about Mattie,' Portia said. 'But you're right Bree. Perhaps another time.'

'My husband's written a book about her,' Ella said. 'Well, it's really about his grandfather who was in the French Resistance during World War Two, but Mattie and his grandfather worked together and were lovers too, so it's just as much her story as his. And it's an incredible one. Made even more exciting by Gill. That's my husband. His name is Guillaume De Fonteneau. He's also written a novel based on Mattie's life. That's under a pen name of M.E.G. Ward, and that's because Mia, Gill and I wrote that one together, so we used our initials, and Mattie's surname was Ward. Okay. Gill wrote most of it. But we did help a bit.'

Mia laughed. 'Too much information, Ella. Sorry, Portia. Ella gets a bit carried away sometimes. But it is a fascinating story and Mattie had an amazing life. Now. You were going to tell us of someone who isn't delighted about your wedding.'

Portia nodded. 'Yes. But I don't blame you for being excited about your husband's books, Ella, and I'll definitely read them. I really do want to hear all about Mattie, and Gill's grandfather and their exploits in the war.' She gave them a genuine smile and took a deep breath. 'Okay. Prior to meeting me, Mikkel was in love with … a married woman. That's not a big deal and it's over, but the thing is, the woman had decided she wanted him back and was planning to leave her

75

husband to be with Mikkel. I won't go into the details. Although no doubt Lilith Shoe will, given half a chance. Anyway, the woman's name is Diana Dunn and her husband is Alex. He was almost killed by his ex-lover at Christmas. Oh dear. There was no need for me to tell you that. I am getting as bad as Lilith. Sorry. Er. Alex and Diana are still together but as recently as last Friday, Diana caused a bit of a scene in The Seahorse Inn. That's Mikkel's pub. I wasn't there so I don't know what happened and all Mikkel will say is exactly what I've said. I was staying with my dad and sister at the time. I'm sure Lilith will fill me in with the details, but I've been avoiding her since I got back.' She gave a small laugh. 'Even diving into shop doorways before she spotted me. Anyway. I'm a little worried that Diana's not taking our engagement and forthcoming wedding well. She might do something else. I just think you need to be aware of that.'

'Diana and Alex Dunn,' Bree said, making more notes. 'Possible concern. Okay. Got that.'

'Wow,' Ella said, refilling her coffee cup. 'Planning this wedding could be more exciting than I thought.'

Seven

A bell tinkled as Tommy opened the door of Seahorse Bites Café. He was still smiling after reading the sign on the glass door. It was a picture of a scruffy-looking dog and it stated, 'Dogs welcome, along with well-behaved humans.'

'Be with you in a jiffy,' a cheery voice called out. 'Sit wherever you like.'

The tone was a cross between a song and a laugh and Tommy recognised it immediately.

'No rush,' he replied, making his way to one of the tables in the window overlooking the sweep of the bay.

The café only had a few other customers but that was probably because it was mid-morning and a week day and most people were either at work or had stayed indoors due to the awful weather. Tommy had arrived in the village last night, in torrential rain but the sun had shown its face this morning. Not for long though, and the weather was even worse now than it had been yesterday.

He shrugged off his waterproof jacket, slung it on the back of the chair and sat down with a huge smile on his face.

The aromas wafting from the kitchen made his stomach rumble and he remembered sitting at a table just like this one, so many years ago now, and ordering poached egg on toast and a pot of tea from the most beautiful woman he had ever seen.

At least he thought so at the time.

That changed when that woman fell in love with someone else and, in turn, after a long while, he fell in love with his first wife.

He'd also met her in this very café where she too had become a waitress along with her best friend, the beautiful waitress, Lyn, whom he was dating by that time.

That relationship didn't last long though once Lyn decided she was in love with another man.

A man who happened to be her best friend's boyfriend.

But that was such a long time ago. And relationships were complicated. He knew that better than most.

After his beloved wife had died, he'd been bereft. His two treasured daughters brought him immense joy, and he threw himself into expanding his hotel empire with even more determination than before. That also gave him pleasure. But his life still felt as though something were missing somehow.

The thing he hated most was retiring to an otherwise empty bed each night. That, he quickly realised, he could remedy, and had done so sooner than he should have.

Every consecutive wife since then had filled the space in his bed, but the hole in his heart was never mended. And eventually he knew it never would be.

He glanced out at the rain and the waves crashing over the circle of rocks in the bay of Seahorse Harbour. Those rocks made up the curl of a seahorse's tail, so Lyn had told him on the first day they had met all those years ago.

There was a rock pool in the centre, large enough to swim in on a warm and sunny day when the tide was out, and the sand surrounding the rocks glistened and sparkled beneath one's toes.

Or on a sultry, summer night, when the water reflected the dark, blue-black velvet-like sky, twinkling with myriad stars, and the full moon seemed to be a ball floating in the middle of that rock pool, whilst two lovers kissed and caressed and made one another promises that one of them wouldn't keep.

He shifted his gaze from outside to in and studied the table where he sat. He wished he could turn the clock back to those days. Not so that he could spend more time with Lyn, or change her mind about him, but so that he could realise sooner that the love of his life was, in fact, her best friend. They would've had more time together if he'd recognised that earlier, and he silently cursed himself for being the fool that he was.

Seconds later, a woman only a few years younger than him appeared from the kitchen. She had a cheerful smile, rosy cheeks, soft, warm blue eyes and tight blonde curls atop a body that to him, looked both attractive and cuddly.

His heart gave an unexpected lurch. She hadn't changed much at all and he wondered if his first beloved wife would have looked just like Lyn did now.

Well, not just like her of course, but similar – and the complete opposite of all his other wives who had been much younger than him, and who didn't have a spare centimetre of flesh between them.

He watched Lyn walk towards him and saw a flicker of recognition in her eyes but she addressed him as she no doubt would all her customers.

'What can I get you, love?'

'Poached egg on toast and a pot of tea, please, Lyn.'

She slowly raised her eyes to his, a frown forming between her brows as she stared at him, her expression slowly softening as realisation dawned and a warm smile replaced the straight line of her lips.

'Tommy?' She sounded both surprised and yet pleased to see him. 'Is it really you?'

He laughed as he nodded. 'It is. You haven't changed at all.'

She laughed too as she tapped him playfully on the shoulder. 'Oh, get away with you. I hardly recognise myself when I look in the mirror.'

'I'd recognise you anywhere. And I mean it. You haven't changed.'

She tipped her head slightly to one side and grinned at him.

'You have. Although I can still see the man I knew beneath that tan, no doubt acquired on some exotic beach, those expensive clothes that I bet cost more than this café is worth and that distinguished-looking head of grey hair which makes mine look like a discarded bird's nest.'

He grinned back at her before getting to his feet and holding open his arms.

'May I?'

Emily Harvale

She laughed louder and nodded, leaning into his hug.

'You may.'

She smelt of lavender and vanilla and also of bacon and eggs all mixed together and he breathed it in as if it were pure, fresh oxygen.

She was still smiling when she eased herself away.

'So what brings you to Seahorse Harbour, Tommy Trulove? And if you say it's me, I'll give you a slap. I suppose you're here to see Portia, aren't you? Are you staying until the wedding, or is this a flying visit?'

'I'm staying for a day or two. Just to get my bearings again after so many years. And I'll be returning in plenty of time for the wedding.' He grinned harder. 'And, at the risk of being slapped, I did come to this café to see you. I could hardly come to Seahorse Harbour and not pop in and say hello, could I?'

'Absolutely not! I'd definitely have given you a slap if I'd heard you were in this neck of the woods and you hadn't come to see me.'

More serious now he asked, 'How are you, Lyn? Is life treating you well? I was sorry to hear of your husband's passing.'

Her smile faded a little too. 'We had many good years. I have to be thankful for that. We were lucky. I was so sad to hear of your loss.'

'Life can be cruel sometimes. At least I have Portia and Bethany to remind me of her. Not that I need reminding. We never really get over those we truly love, do we?'

Lyn shook her head. 'No, we don't. They say time heals but it's not true. It merely softens the pain. I still find myself wondering what he might have said or done in any given situation.'

'I'm the same. But unlike you, I tried to ease the pain by marrying again.' He laughed joylessly. 'Several times, in fact. It doesn't work.'

She frowned at him. 'That's because from what I've seen and heard, you've been marrying all the wrong people. It seems to me you've been looking for the complete opposite of what you had. That's never going to bring you happiness, Tommy.'

He shrugged. 'I know. Perhaps we only get one true love in our lives.'

'Or perhaps you're too frightened to fall in love again so you pick women you know you'll never really love.'

He held her gaze and a grin formed again. 'Even after all these years, you know me so well.'

She studied his face in silence for a moment.

'Maybe you're right, Tommy. Maybe we haven't changed at all. I know I'll never love anyone as much as I did my husband, but I also know I'd like to find love again. Or perhaps just a very good friendship. I've got good friends here and of course I've got my wonderful nephew, Nathan who lives with me now. And he's just got engaged to a lovely young woman named Sorcha. But it's not the same, is it? Not like having someone special to sit quietly with of an evening. Or to listen to music with, or go for a stroll with along the sand.'

'No. It isn't.'

'Oh goodness. Will you listen to us! We're getting all nostalgic.'

'There's nothing wrong with nostalgia. It's self-pity that's a problem.'

She raised her brows. 'Don't tell me you feel sorry for yourself, Tommy Trulove because that I won't believe.'

He let out a sigh. 'I've got more money than I know what to do with. Two wonderful daughters I adore. A rather great, soon-to-be son-in-law. A hugely successful business. I've got everything most people could ever dream of. Except one thing. I don't have that special someone to share any of it with anymore. And no matter how many wives I have, I don't think I ever will again.'

'Do you know what I dream about?' Lyn sat down at the table and he sat opposite. 'I always wanted to travel. We had holidays. Lots of them. And they were fabulous. But I always thought that one day we'd retire and travel the world. I wanted to go on one of those world cruises, you know.'

'You still could, couldn't you?'

'Yes. And now would be the perfect time. Nathan can run this place with his eyes closed, even though he's actually just started his own business. He's an architect and a damned good one and he left a major firm to come and help me out. But I knew it wouldn't be long before he wanted to set something up of his own and he has my blessing. I could get someone else to run the café, but as luck would have it, Sorcha, his fiancée was born to do this.' Lyn leant forward and grinned. 'She's never really been able to settle at a job. Or a relationship, but that's another story, and before she realised she was mad about Nathan. Now she's found her niche, not just in love but here. She reminds me of me when I was her age.'

'So you're planning to retire?'

Lyn pulled a face. 'Not really. I could. I'd like to. But I don't know what I'd do without this place. And all my memories are here.'

'You can take your memories with you. Believe me, I know.' He leant back against the chair and stretched out his long legs beside the table. 'What about the world cruise?'

Lyn shook her head. 'I wouldn't want to do that on my own. Oh, I know I would meet people and I'm sure it'd be a lot of fun, but I'm not one of those women who can just go off on her own adventure. It's silly, I know. But I think I'd be lonely.'

'It's not silly at all. And I completely understand. I often feel lonely, even though I've got my darling daughters. I have lots of acquaintances and some people I would call my friends, but not the sort of friends that really know me. Not like we all knew one another in the old days.'

'I think that too. It's as if the friendships we made back then were special in some way.'

'I think they were, Lyn. I think they were very special.'

Their gaze held until the bell over the door tinkled and Lyn shot to her feet.

'Goodness me. I completely forgot where I was. And didn't you order tea and egg on toast at least ten minutes ago? I'll get that right away.' She shot a look towards the door and smiled, her eyes opening wide as if in surprise. 'Hello, loves. Sit anywhere you like. I'll be with you in a jiffy.' She returned her gaze to Tommy and her smile told him everything he needed to know. 'And as for you, Tommy, we've got a lot of catching up to do.'

With that, she dashed off to the kitchen and the door swung shut behind her.

Eight

'Why can't we sit by the window?' Ella moaned as Bree led the way to a table in a cosy corner of Seahorse Bites Café.

'Because the three of us will have to move the other tables just to fit in,' Bree replied. 'And besides, every time the door opens, we'll feel the force of that wind, and I'm already shivering. I knew I shouldn't have listened to you. "It won't rain", you said. "You don't need to take your mac, just your fold-up jacket." And now it's pelting down and freezing cold, so thanks for that.'

Ella grinned as they sat down. 'Anytime. But don't blame me. You didn't have to take any notice. And I'm drenched too.'

Mia laughed, taking off her raincoat and hanging it on a hook on the wall beside their table.

'Jet told me when he phoned this morning that it would definitely rain today. Farmers always know what the weather's going to do. Even my phone forecast rain, so I don't know why you two thought it wouldn't pour hard.'

'It was sunny this morning!' Bree declared in her defence. 'We sat outside and had breakfast in bright sunshine. And Ella convinced me, even after the sun went in, I'd only end up lugging my mac around in the heat.'

'Shush,' Mia said, placing the tip of her forefinger on her mouth. 'That waitress is coming over and we don't want to seem like squabbling teenagers.'

'She started it,' Ella quipped, winking at Mia.

'I did not,' Bree whispered.

'Is there an expectant mothers' convention in the village I don't know about?'

Bree stared at the waitress for a second before returning the woman's grin. 'Oh. Because you don't usually get three pregnant women in here at the same time, you mean?'

'Not ever. As far as I can recall. I'm Lyn. What can I get you, my loves? You look like you need a towel. I'll get you one in a jiffy.'

Bree liked Lyn's smile, and the woman's voice had a cheery ring to it.

'I'm starving,' Ella said.

Bree tutted. 'How can you be starving? We only had breakfast two hours ago.'

'I need a slice of chocolate cake, if you have that, please,' said Mia. 'And a pot of tea.'

'I've got chocolate cake to die for,' Lyn said. 'Bev, who owns Beach Bakers next door, makes it and no one can resist it.'

'Better make it two slices then, please.'

Ella cast Mia an admonishing look. 'Two slices of cake. Really? You're already the size of a house.'

Mia stuck out her chin. 'I'm adding an extension.'

Ella snorted with laughter. 'Oh well. I may as well join you. But only one slice for me. A large slice, please. And I'll also have a pot of tea, thanks.'

'Just a cup of lemon and ginger herbal tea for me, please,' Bree said. 'If you have that.'

Mia and Ella exchanged glances.

'You're in luck,' Lyn said. 'Only two weeks ago my nephew's fiancée suggested we stock herbal teas. I'm sure lemon and ginger was one of them. Right. I'll be back in a jiffy with that towel.'

'What?' Bree glared at Mia and Ella as Lyn hurried away. 'I'm taking care of myself.'

Ella rolled her eyes. 'Yeah right. Let me guess. You spoke to Garrick after breakfast and he reminded you to eat and drink sensibly, didn't he?' She leant back in her chair and turned her head. 'Excuse me, Lyn. Our friend wants chocolate cake too.'

'Right you are, love.'

Bree opened her mouth to argue but closed it again. Ella was right on all counts. Garrick had phoned after breakfast, and he had reminded her to "watch what you eat because you don't want to get indigestion". He meant well, and he only had her welfare at heart, but sometimes he could be a bit of a killjoy. And Bree did want chocolate cake. Very much so.

'Fine,' she said, after giving the matter a bit of thought. 'But only because Bev is the woman who'll be making the cake for the wedding, so this'll be a good opportunity to try out her baking.'

'Er. Aren't we going for a taster session at 3.00 this afternoon?' Ella asked, looking a little concerned.

'We are,' Bree said. 'But she's expecting us then so she might make more of an effort. This way we can see what her cakes are usually like.'

Ella frowned. 'What? Because you think she only makes an effort when she wants to get business but once she's got it, her cakes go downhill? That doesn't make any sense. She'd lose customers if she did that.

Sometimes I wonder about you, Bree. Really I do.'

'What else is on the 'To Do' list today, Bree?' Mia asked, shaking her head at Ella. 'I'm looking forward to meeting Mikkel along with Portia's family at lunch but didn't you say we're going somewhere else first? I've forgotten already. My memory's like a sieve these days.'

'The church. We need to see that and also meet the Reverend.' She lowered her voice so that the other customers in the café couldn't hear. 'Portia's meeting us there at 11.30 after her business meeting at that other place she mentioned.'

'I remember that!' Mia said. 'The Seahorse Harbour Holiday Park. I can't believe she met her future husband because they both wanted that site. And now they're building a luxury eco hotel together.' She let out a swoony sigh.

'Actually,' Ella said, 'she told us she met him when she nearly ran him over. And as for the hotel, it's still an eco hotel, so I'm not sure how luxurious it'll be in spite of what she said. Plus they're not building it. They've got people to do that. They'll just stand around and supervise.'

'Don't you like her?' Bree asked. 'That had an edge of bitchiness.'

Ella shrugged. 'I don't know her. I like that she's paying for everything we want at the hotel. But then again that's a pittance to her, isn't it? And I like that she arranged a minicab to bring us here from the hotel. She seemed okay when we met this morning. But I'm not sure who's organising this wedding. You or her. I couldn't believe it when she handed you that itinerary for today and expected us to fit in with the plans she'd made.'

'Oh, Ella. She said we could change any or all of it if we wanted to. She only did that because she's eager to get the cake booked, and for us to see the church so that we can place an order with the florist for the church flowers. And we do need to get the invitations sent out without delay, so the meeting today about that is absolutely necessary. And as we're doing that over lunch, I would've thought you'd be pleased about that bit.'

'Yeah, yeah. And to book the marquees and the string quartet or whatever, and the DJ, and the lighting firm, and the horse and carriage and, on and on and on. I get it. Everything's urgent. But you're the wedding planner. Not her. If she is going to do all this herself then why does she need you? Just to nod and tell her how wonderful all her ideas and suggestions are? Because that's what you did, you know. And you've got much better ideas than she has. I don't understand why you didn't speak up.'

Bree sighed. 'Because she was really excited this morning and I didn't want to dampen her enthusiasm. This is her wedding. Not mine. And even though she was rushing off to her other meeting, she came all the way to our hotel just to be welcoming, and stopped to have breakfast with us. I think that was a lovely thing to do. I'll make some suggestions when we meet later. I know what I'm doing, Ella. This isn't my first wedding, you know.'

'Yes,' Mia said. 'And I seem to recall a certain someone being far worse than that when that someone asked Bree to arrange her wedding last year. Not naming any names, Mrs Ella De Fonteneau.'

'What? Me?' Ella raised her brows. 'I was the perfect client.'

'You were a perfect nightmare,' Bree said. 'It's a good thing we love you. Let's just see how things go, shall we? We all want it to be a fantastic wedding and for the day to go off without a hitch. And she did say she was open to any and all suggestions.'

'Fine,' Ella continued. 'I can't wait to meet the fiancé in the flesh. He looked bloody gorgeous in those photos she showed us on her phone. A tall, blond, broad-shouldered Viking and a sexy hunk of a man.

I almost gave birth just looking at him on the screen.'

'Don't say that to Gill,' Bree advised.

Ella rolled her eyes. 'I'm not a complete idiot. He's already getting a bit weird and I've only been gone for one night. When he called me just now as we were getting out of the minicab, he said he couldn't find his laptop charger. Or his special mug. And he asked me if I'd taken them.' She tutted loudly. 'As if I would've, right? I've got my own charger. And I bought him that mug as a gift, so I'd never take it from him. Besides, why would I want to bring a mug with the words, "Writer's rocket fuel" emblazoned across the front, to a five-star hotel that has posh, and rather beautiful, porcelain cups? The man's mad. He said he wondered if I'd picked up his charger as well as mine, and whether I'd taken the mug in case I missed him.' She let out a sigh. 'See. Totally insane.'

'Perhaps that's just his way of saying he misses you,' Bree suggested.

'Nope. I wouldn't be surprised if it were his way of saying that I've been behaving like a complete moron yet again. He's been saying stuff like that quite a lot over the last few months. I know I've been a little forgetful – although nowhere near as bad as Mia – and okay, I've had a few mood swings now and again. And yes, a couple of months ago, I did manage to somehow erase half of the new book he was working on, meaning he had to rewrite it all. But it's not my fault. It's my hormones.'

'Hmmm.' Mia placed a hand on Ella's arm. 'Don't shout at me for saying this, but I've been holding this back for way too long. You're the one who's totally insane, Ella. Don't give me that glowering look. You've been more than forgetful, and you know it. And your mood swings have been off the chart. I've known you all my life and I've never seen you like this. I've told you that already. But when you lost half his book, did he shout and scream and throw things in a temper tantrum? Nope. That was you. He was the epitome of calm and collected and he forgave you immediately and assured you it wasn't the end of the world. I'm not sure what's going on with you and whenever I ask, you merely shrug and say "It's my hormones". Well, Bree and I have hormones too and we're not raving loonies. That's one of the reasons I thought this was a good idea. Maybe a few days away from Gill would make you open up to me. And to Bree. And tell us what the problem is. Because there clearly is one, isn't there?'

'Ella?' Bree coaxed. 'Mia's right. I have to agree. You have been behaving a little strangely. Or perhaps I should say, stranger than usual.'

Ella's frown slowly faded but her eyes were now cast down and her shoulders hunched.

'I know. But I don't know why. I do think it's my hormones … or something.' She raised her eyes and smiled wanly. 'The truth is, the closer I get to being a mum, the more terrified I feel. I'm not convinced I'm ready for this. I can't even look after myself properly half the time so how am I supposed to look after a baby? And then I feel useless. You make it look so easy, Bree. And I know you'll be a fantastic mum, Mia. But I'm a bit of a mess at the best of times, and this won't come naturally to me. What if I screw up?'

'Oh Ella, you won't,' Mia sympathised, squeezing Ella's arm. 'I'm terrified too, you know. I may not say so and I may pretend it's all fine, but the thought of being responsible for three living, breathing babies is very scary. But I know Jet will be brilliant and that comforts me. Gill will be brilliant too, Ella, so he'll pick up any slack there might be, just like Jet will for me. And you may not think you'll be a natural at this, but you will. Honestly, you will.'

'Absolutely,' said Bree. 'And let's face it, Ella. You know more about behaving like a child than we do, so you'll have perfect empathy with your baby.' She reached out and touched Ella's hand, beaming at her as she did so.

Ella brightened a little. 'Gill will be great, won't he? And you're right about me being a kid, Bree. I shouldn't see it as a negative, more as a bonus. Plus, I know you have far more reason to feel anxious than me, Mia. I mean three babies! God. I'm terrified at the thought of having one. It's stupid, I know. But sometimes I think this is a big mistake and I wish I could turn the clock back to the days when I could drink as much as I wanted and have sex with anyone I wanted and do anything I wanted. Now I've got to take care of someone else for the rest of my life. And that's a daunting and very sobering prospect, in more ways than one.'

'I think the same, sometimes,' Mia said. 'Then I look at Jet and my heart almost bursts from my chest with the love I feel for him. We all go through this, Ella. We all have doubts and fears. It's only natural. And I look like a whale. Or a house as you're always telling me, and I wonder how Jet can still look at me as if I'm the most beautiful woman on the planet. But he does. And Gill looks at you in the same way.'

Ella shrugged. 'Maybe. When he's not staring at his bloody laptop screen all day and all night for weeks on end.'

'Are you saying he's not paying you enough attention?' Bree asked. 'If that's the case, just tell him.'

'How can I? I'm the one who erased the damn book in the first place, so it's my fault he's now on a nightmare of a deadline to get it done in time.'

'Ella De Fonteneau!' Mia said, exasperation evident in her tone. 'You really are insane. Your happiness means far more to Gill than any book or deadline. You know that. If this is really all that's bothering you, then I agree with Bree. Just tell him.'

'Yeah. And then feel even more guilty? Right. Good thinking.' She shook her head. 'I know, I know. I told you it was silly. But I can't help the way I feel. This week will give him the time he needs to finish it, I hope, and then we'll see. Ah. Here's our chocolate cake. Let's enjoy this and forget about me and Gill and what's happening in Little Pondale, shall we? Let's focus on this wedding and making it the best one yet. But I'm telling you right now. I don't care what's on that bloody itinerary for today. After we've met Bev at Beach Bakers, I'm heading for the hotel, and spending several hours in the spa.'

Nine

It was still pouring with rain when Bree, Mia and Ella finally left Seahorse Bites Café. The wind had picked up substantially resulting in the large umbrella Lyn had lent them, quickly losing its battle with the elements. But at least it was an on-shore wind, which meant that once they'd navigated their way along Sea Walk and turned into Sand Lane, they were virtually blown up the hill to their destination.

Although as they hurried past The Seahorse Inn at the top of Sand Lane, they exchanged glances, each of them being sorely tempted to take shelter inside the village pub. But the church was just across the road, so they resisted and continued on.

St Mary Star of the Sea was undeniably bijou, just as Portia had told them, and ancient too. Norman, Portia had said. That was evident the moment they laid eyes on it. The square, dumpy tower at one end had large and rather magnificent stained-glass windows, and an equally large but not quite so magnificent, white-faced clock. Behind the church, and only just visible from where they stood, was a tiny graveyard, the gravestones of which looked almost as old as the church.

The church and graveyard sat on what was effectively a slightly raised 'island' surrounded by three roads; Church Row, which contained a row of shops and a cluster of cottages and led up towards Seahorse Cliffs; Meadow Lane, to the right which contained a row of colourful cottages as pretty as a summer meadow, and to the left, Church Hill, which led up to a couple of houses and a number of fields, and down in the other direction to Sea Walk.

Opposite the church and on the corner of Church Hill and Wood Lane sat a building called The Olde Forge where Fulbright Ceramics was situated, as Ella pointed out.

'That's where Lyn told us that gorgeous seahorse of hers came from,' she said, as the three of them stood beneath the wooden lychgate at the entrance to the church, which, along with a massive and also ancient oak situated to one side of that, offered them some protection from the wind and rain.

Although the bright yellow bench in front of the tree was taking quite a battering, not just from the elements but also from the bowing branches whipping against it.

'Wonderful,' Bree said. 'We can go in there another time. Let's get inside the church and out of this awful weather. I'm saturated yet again.'

Bree would've loved to have spent an hour or so browsing in Fulbright Ceramics, having looked at the leaflet Lyn had produced from her apron pocket and handed to them as she'd brought their drinks and the chocolate cake – which Bree later had to concede was possibly the best she'd ever tasted. But now wasn't the time to shop for pottery and the like. They were meeting Portia and the vicar at 11.30, and thanks to Garrick calling to check that Bree "had worn her coat" and that "things were going well" they were already five minutes late. She'd lied to him about her coat, and he'd sussed it, so she had then had to placate him for having fibbed, and that had taken far longer than it should have.

They raced as fast as they could, taking care not to slip on the path from the gate to the church and Mia shoved the solid oak door open with the full force of her body, almost careering into a slightly overweight woman with short, spiky, white-blonde hair who was opening the door from the inside.

'I'm so sorry,' Mia said, managing to keep her balance and not land in the woman's arms. 'The door was stiff and I had to shove it open.'

The woman beamed at her. 'Yes. Sorry about that. It does that when the weather's like this. I'm Persephone, the Reverend, but everyone calls me Perse. Portia's not ... ah. Here she is.'

Portia dashed in behind them just as Bree was attempting to push the heavy door shut.

'Perfect timing, Portia,' Perse said. 'But goodness gracious. You're all soaked. Come into the church hall and I'll get you some towels. We can do the introductions once you're not dripping quite so much.'

Her laughter rang out like a peal of bells as they all smiled at one another and followed Perse around the wood pews towards a heavy, red velvet curtain, behind which, another door creaked open. This led into a small, wooden hall that was much newer than the church, by several centuries, but still looked as if it was from another time. Possibly the early 1930s or thereabouts.

Tables and chairs that had also been around for some considerable time by the looks of them were stacked against the walls, and the plain but faded wood floor was in want of a good polish. The windows, rattling as the weather pounded them, could do with a clean, but the hall was warm and dry and oddly welcoming.

'Grab some chairs for our guests, Portia and I'll get the towels,' Perse said, disappearing into a small room at one end.

Bree and the others went to get their own chairs but Portia stopped them.

'I'll do that.' She placed one chair after another in a sort of rough circle and then picked up a table, nearly toppling over as she did so. Ella grabbed the legs and helped her balance it. 'Thanks. That would've been great if I'd ended up under a table and without even having a glass of wine,' Portia joked.

Perse returned with a couple of hand towels, two tea towels and a wad of paper napkins.

'Best I could do, I'm afraid, but I have put the kettle on in the kitchen, so at least we can have a hot drink.'

Mia and Portia weren't as soaked as Ella and Bree, both having been sensible enough to wear macs and not simply fold-away jackets, so they took the paper napkins, leaving the towels for Ella and Bree.

It only took a moment or two for them all to remove the excess water, and a beaming Perse tossed the sodden bundle of towels and napkins into two separate plastic bags she'd been holding.

'Right,' she said. 'Who wants tea and who wants coffee? That's all I can offer, sadly.'

Everyone wanted tea, so that was fairly simple, and a few minutes later, Perse carried a tray of steaming mugs to the table in the centre of the circle Portia had made.

'Thanks, Perse,' Portia said. 'Now it's time for the introductions. This is Bree, my wedding planner and these are Mia and Ella, her best friends and, I believe she said, "best assistants". Ladies, this is Perse, the Reverend of St Mary Star of the Sea.'

They all exchanged the usual pleasantries and discussed the appalling weather over their mugs of tea.

'You'd never believe it was June,' Perse said. 'I've got two weddings this weekend and a christening tomorrow. I'm hoping the weather will change and I've asked the appropriate person to do his bit.' She raised her eyes towards the ceiling, no doubt referring to the heavens. 'But let's chat about Portia and Mikkel's Big Day, shall we? What do you need from me, Bree?'

'Nothing, really,' Bree said, 'other than access to the church for the florist, and, of course, for the rehearsal. We haven't yet discussed music, so we'll need to sort that out. Obviously, the church is too small to have an organ so I assume most of your weddings use pre-recorded music.'

Perse nodded. 'We do have bells though. They're not pre-recorded. But the bellringers need to be booked if you want the real thing, which I'd definitely advise. Nothing quite like a peal of bells at a wedding.'

'Oh yes,' Portia said. 'We definitely want real bells.'

Perse smiled. 'I thought you might from our previous chats. I'll get in touch with the group, Bree and I'll give you their details.'

Bree made a note on her phone. 'Okay. Thanks for that. Now, some brides like to have a musical ensemble, or even a small choir. Some have a single harpist, or a violin quartet, or something along those lines. Others use the pre-recorded music. Have you thought about what you want, Portia?'

Portia screwed up her face. 'Definitely not pre-recorded, if possible. I know stuff like The Wedding March would probably sound better on an organ, or if pre-recorded, and that having singers, or musicians might not have such an impact, but I'm not really sure what I want to walk down the aisle to. I keep changing my mind. I've discussed it with Mikkel and he's happy with whatever I want. Dad and my sister, Bethany say the same. My best friend, Angela has said that I should choose something that means a lot to me and that I don't need to have anything traditional if I don't want to. But that wasn't as much help as she thought it was. Because I still don't know what I want.'

Bree smiled in understanding. 'If you do want anything other than pre-recorded music, I'm sorry to say you will need to decide fairly soon. All the best musicians – and I only use the best – do tend to get booked up. Some are already completely booked for this year and next, and don't have a space for even one more wedding. But there are always ways around it, so don't panic. The important thing is for you to decide what would make the day that little bit extra special for you. I'm happy to make suggestions but let's leave that for now and we can come back to it later. Possibly over lunch, if that gives you enough time to decide. The only issue, as far as Perse is concerned, is where to put whatever or whoever you decide to have. Okay. Flowers. Is there a local florist you want to use?'

By the time Bree had gone through the list, the rain had finally stopped and they all walked from the church into bright sunshine.

'Well, that's a good sign,' Ella said.

'Let's hope everything continues that way,' added Portia. 'Now it's sunny, are you okay to walk up to Mikkel's for lunch? It's just a little way up the hill. You can see his house from here. It's that big one standing near the edge of the cliffs.'

'Wow,' Bree said. 'That's one impressive house.'

Portia beamed and blushed with pride. 'And so is the man who owns it.'

Ten

'Mikkel, Dad, Bethany,' Portia said, as she led Bree, Mia and Ella into Mikkel's sitting room. 'This is Bree, my wedding planner, and Mia and Ella, her friends and assistants.'

'Lovely to meet you.' Mikkel stepped forward and greeted each of the women in turn with a semi-formal handshake. 'Welcome to my ... I mean, *our* home.' He gave one of his melodic laughs that Portia loved so much. 'I'm still getting used to the fact that Portia said 'yes' and made me the happiest man in the world just a few weeks ago. Or perhaps I should say, one of the happiest men. Your three partners must feel the same. I hope my darling fiancée will give you all some time to rest and relax.' He winked at Portia. 'But I know how kind and thoughtful she is so I have no doubts on that score.'

He stepped back in order for the others to say hello and Tommy patted Mikkel on the back and smiled at him.

Portia loved the fact that her dad and her fiancé had hit it off the moment they met, just seven weeks ago, which was shortly after Mikkel proposed.

Portia had already told her dad and her sister that she had fallen in love with Mikkel but both of them were more than a little surprised when she announced they'd got engaged.

Their reaction was completely understandable and she was still a little surprised herself at the time. She'd only met Mikkel five days beforehand. To say it was a whirlwind romance was a bit of an understatement.

But she hadn't had the slightest doubt that Mikkel was 'The One'. She'd known it the moment she'd almost hit him with her car. Their eyes had met as he sat upright on that grassy verge and it was as if her heart had leapt out of her body and thrown itself into his arms. It hadn't taken her many hours for her to throw the rest of her body into those strong, tanned arms.

Luckily, both her dad and Bethany trusted her judgement on all things. Although her dad did keep asking her why she was rushing to get married. But not because he didn't like Mikkel. It was only because he wanted her to have her dream wedding and he was concerned that if she rushed things, she might regret it later.

This wedding was going to be far smaller than it would have been if she had held the ceremony in London. The guest list had already been cut twice and now only close friends and family of the bride and groom were being invited.

Her dad had been concerned about that but Portia had assured him that this was what she wanted. All the pomp and ceremony of a wedding like the Tuffet bash was not for her.

In truth, if she had her way, she and Mikkel would have jumped on a plane and had their nuptials on the sandy shore of an island in the South Pacific, possibly beneath a swaying, coconut palm. The island of Bora Bora perhaps, where it just so happened there was a rather luxurious, Trulove hotel.

But she knew Mikkel wanted his friends in Seahorse Harbour to attend and that a trip to the Society Islands wasn't possible for many of them, even if she had offered to cover all the costs, so she had kept that particular wish to herself. Mikkel's friends all had businesses to run and they couldn't simply up and leave at the drop of a hat.

'I'm Tommy,' her dad said, smiling at Bree and her friends as he too, introduced himself with a handshake. 'It's good to meet you all. I saw you in Seahorse Bites Café this morning but I had no idea who you were or I would've come over and introduced myself.'

Bree darted a look at her friends and her smile seemed a little nervous.

'You ... you were in the café? Oh dear. I mean. Oh dear, what a shame we didn't realise who you were. We would've said hello. Er. I think I remember seeing you now. You were sitting at one of the tables in the window over the other side of the café.'

'I was.' He winked at Bree and smiled at all three women. 'But don't worry. I couldn't hear a thing you said.'

'Oh.' Bree sounded almost relieved as she let out a breath.

Ella burst out laughing. 'Busted!' she said, as she shook Tommy's hand. 'Did you have any of the chocolate cake? It was the best I've ever had. And believe me that's high praise, because Jenny, our friend who owns Lake's Bakes in Little Pondale makes heavenly cakes. Oh. Heavenly cakes!' She looked at Bree and Mia and laughed louder.

'Sorry about her,' Mia said, grinning. 'She's laughing because she said "Heavenly", and Jenny Lake, who owns Lake's Bakes is marrying Glen Fox later this year. He's the vicar of our village church, St Michael and All Angels. Ella's got an odd sense of humour.'

'No, I haven't,' Ella said.

Tommy smiled as he shook Mia's hand. 'She'll need it, planning my daughter's wedding.' He beamed at Portia. 'Only joking, sweetheart.'

'He's right though,' Bethany said, giving a little wave from where she stood. 'I'm Bethany, the baby sister. I adore Portia, but she likes to get her own way and can be "as stubborn as a mule", as Dad would say.'

'Hey!' Portia laughed. 'Okay. That's true. Bethany's my maid of honour.'

'And her best friend, Angela, is her matron of honour,' Bethany added, grinning. 'See what I mean? Most brides only have one maid or matron of honour. Portia wants two.'

'Only because I love you both so much and you're equally special to me, but in different ways. I want you both by my side on my Big Day.'

'And we're both thrilled and honoured.' Bethany made a playful curtesy.

Tommy gave a roar of laughter. 'And you think Ella's got an odd sense of humour. Meet my daughters.'

'What can I get you to drink?' Mikkel asked. 'And please come and sit down.'

'I'd like a large glass of red wine,' Ella said, pulling a face. 'Sadly though, I can't have one. Anything non-alcoholic is fine with me, thanks. And that's a sentence I'll never get the hang of saying.'

Everyone laughed at that as Bree, Mia and Ella all sat on one of the large sofas whilst Bethany and Tommy sat on another.

While Mikkel asked Bree and Mia about drinks, Portia poured Tommy a glass of whisky and was about to pour herself a glass of wine, but thought better of it.

'What about mocktails?' Mikkel asked. 'I do own a pub and a restaurant so I can make a pretty good mocktail even if I say so myself.'

'Yes please,' Ella said, and so did Bree and Mia.

'I'll have one too,' Portia said, 'and I'll get you a beer from the fridge while you make them.'

'And me,' added Bethany. 'A mocktail, that is. Not a beer.' She shivered dramatically. 'I don't get what people like about beer. It's just another form of watered-down porridge if you ask me. It's all made from oats. And who wants to drink that? Yuk.'

'Actually, that's not true...' Mikkel let his voice trail off and he beamed at Bethany. 'You're just winding me up, aren't you?'

Bethany shrugged. 'Yeah. But I really don't like beer. Or lager.' She winked at him.

'Have you already divided up duties?' Bree asked, when Portia returned with Mikkel's beer. 'Between the maid and matron of honour? Or would you like me to do that?'

Portia glanced at both Bree and Bethany as Mikkel handed out the mocktails he'd made. 'Er. No, I haven't.'

Each drink was in a rainbow-effect, Margarita-glass and each had a different coloured glass cocktail stick with a gorgeous parrot at its tip. He began with the guests before returning to Portia. She took hers from him as he kissed her on the cheek.

'We have duties?' Bethany asked, taking her drink from Mikkel a moment later. 'I thought we were just meant to walk down the aisle in stunningly gorgeous dresses. We actually have to do stuff?'

Ella winked. 'A girl after my own heart. It came as a shock to me when my friend Mia got married.'

Bree tutted at Ella and smiled reassuringly at Bethany. 'A wedding involves a great deal of hard work. It comes as a surprise to a lot of people. But it is fun too. And besides, Portia has us, so we'll do most if not all of it. You can do as much or as little as you want. Although, as I can see by your face, you were probably just teasing your sister.'

'Yeah,' Bethany said. 'I was. I thought I'd have to do something and I'm more than happy to, but other than us going and picking the wedding dress, she didn't tell me what.'

'Because I don't know,' Portia said. 'This is my first time as a bride-to-be, and although I was a bridesmaid at Angela's wedding, I can't remember what I did. Other than drink an awful lot of champagne and laugh because Angela couldn't. She was pregnant at the time. I think her wedding planner did everything and just gave me a list of 'dos and don'ts', none of which I can recall.'

Bethany laughed. 'We should've paid more attention at one of Dad's weddings. Although all the bridezillas kept us at a distance. Oops. Sorry, Dad.'

Tommy smiled at Bethany, shook his head and shrugged.

'What can I say? There have been a lot. But I'm not sure I paid that much attention either, now I come to think of it.'

'Oh, Dad,' Portia said. 'Er. I suppose we should explain.' She smiled at Bree, Mia and Ella. 'Our mum died when we were young, and Dad ... well, Dad missed her terribly. As we all did.'

'But unlike my daughters, I attempted to find comfort by trying to fill the massive hole in my heart, and like the fool that I can be when it comes to Love, I thought taking another wife might help with that even though I knew that no one could, or ever would, replace my beloved wife. It's taken me several more marriages to realise that I'll never find comfort that way. How many is it now? I've lost track myself.'

'Five, since Mum died.' Portia couldn't stop the sigh of sadness escaping.

'Five? Is it really? Yes. I suppose it is. Clearly, I'm a slow learner.' Tommy's sigh was even sadder.

'And not one remains on our Christmas card list,' Bethany said, with an oddly cheerful smile. 'But at least the parties were good. Oooh! A party! Can I organise the bridal shower? Please, Portia. Please. Angela can arrange the hen party.'

'Gosh. I hadn't even thought about those.' Portia looked at Bree. 'Is there time?'

Bree nodded. 'We can make time, if that's what you want. Some brides-to-be have both. Some, just the one. A bridal shower is another thing we've adopted from across the pond.'

'Any excuse for a party,' Ella said. 'I had both last year. Not that I can remember much about either. It was in the heady days before I got pregnant and I was still allowed to drink.' Her sigh was both wistful and melancholic but she quickly brightened up.

'And this mocktail is divine. Almost as good as real alcohol. Any chance of getting the recipe, Mikkel?'

'Of course. I'll write it down for you.'

'Excellent. Thanks.'

Mikkel smiled at Portia. 'You're welcome to have the pub, the restaurant, or the nightclub for either, if that helps. Or for both. I promise to stay out of the way on each occasion.'

Portia beamed at him. 'That's a brilliant idea. Thank you.' She turned to Bree. 'I told you Mikkel owned a pub, restaurant and nightclub, didn't I?'

Bree nodded and a massive smile spread across her face. 'That would make booking the venues so much easier.'

Mikkel laughed. 'I'll only charge half the usual price.'

'That had better be a joke,' Bethany said, laughing too. 'Or you'll be looking for a new fiancée.'

'I rather like the one I've got.' Mikkel reached out for Portia, pulling her into his arms. 'And she can have anything of mine for free.'

Eleven

'It was good of Mikkel to offer to drive to Easterhill just to post the invitations this afternoon,' Bree said, as she, Portia, Bethany, Mia and Ella walked down Church Row later that afternoon and turned into Sand Lane to keep their appointment with Bev at Beach Bakers.

Portia nodded. 'He's keen to help. It means he'll be able to catch the late afternoon collection so the invitations should all arrive tomorrow, or Saturday at the latest. As we're short of time, even one day makes a difference for the few people we haven't been able to email or contact via any other means.' She laughed. 'Although he definitely wasn't keen to spend an hour tasting wedding cakes, so I think the offer to drive to Easterhill was more as a way of getting out of this.'

Most of the invitations either had, or were, being emailed out by Bethany, and also by Angela from her own home, or sent via social media, so getting the handwritten invitations posted, wasn't imperative. But there were a few people whose only contact details were a postal address, and besides, Portia and Mikkel wanted all their guests to have a keepsake — one of the beautifully crafted invitations that she had already ordered and that she and Mikkel had written out. They were cut from handmade paper embedded with rose petals that had been added to the pulp in the papermaking process and each one was edged with gold leaf. Another thing that had been produced locally, by someone Mikkel knew.

'I thought all bridegrooms were supposed to try out the cakes,' Bethany said, laughing too. 'I'm surprised you let him off so easily.'

'Keep this a secret between all of us,' Portia said, 'but I'm glad he didn't want to come. I absolutely adore him, and I know I haven't known him long, but one thing I do know is if he'd come with us this afternoon he'd have chosen the first cake we tasted and would've asked why we needed to taste more than that. When it comes to cakes, he likes them all, even though he says he doesn't really have a sweet tooth. I assure you, that's a lie. Although I think he believes it. The point is, he doesn't have a favourite and he'd say each one he tried was the best so he'd never actually pick one over another. Which sort of defeats the object of the exercise. This way, I'll be able to choose something I know we'll both be happy with. We've already agreed what we want it to look like and how many tiers it should have.'

Bree was beginning to wonder why Portia needed her at all.

Portia had already purchased her wedding dress and the dresses for Bethany and Angela; the invitations were now done and dusted with no input from Bree – other than to say how beautiful they were when she was shown them over lunch. The church was booked prior to Bree's arrival in Seahorse Harbour and although she had met the Reverend that morning and made a few suggestions regarding the order of service, most of it had already been agreed between Portia, Mikkel and Perse when Portia and Mikkel had booked the church the week before.

The marquees for Mikkel's spacious garden were also booked and would be arriving and erected two days prior to the wedding; the menus for the wedding breakfast at Mikkel's restaurant, Hippocampus; the informal lunch for the residents of the village at The Seahorse Inn and the evening sit-down meal in the marquees for the wedding guests were all but finalised.

Portia also knew exactly what she wanted when it came to the flowers. She said she'd hoped to use a local florist but some of the blooms she'd chosen were rather exotic so Tommy decreed during lunch that the florists they used for the Trulove Hotels would also supply the wedding flowers, bouquets and boutonnières. Bree did say the florists on her lists could easily meet Portia's needs, but once Tommy had spoken, there seemed little point.

It didn't really leave that much for Bree and her team to do. Apart from follow up on everything and ensure it all went to plan. Bree could do that from her cottage in Little Pondale. But she'd wait for a day or two and see how things progressed. She might be called on to sort something out that Portia hadn't considered, or mediate with suppliers when things went wrong as she knew from experience, happened more than most people imagined. Which was why they hired wedding planners.

Beach Bakers was exactly as Portia had described it and Bev, the owner was lovely. Bree already knew Bev's chocolate cake was scrumptious but she couldn't believe how delicious every other variety of cake was that they tried. She wouldn't dream of telling Jenny of Lake's Bakes, back in Little Pondale, but Bev's cakes equalled Jenny's in each case and one or two might even have edged into prime position as far as Bree's tastebuds were concerned.

They'd arrived at 3.00 and had tasted more cakes than even Mia or Ella could manage but Portia had decided what she wanted within the first ten minutes. After that, all the tastings had simply been to make certain there wasn't something better than the ones Portia had selected.

Wasn't that precisely what Portia had said Mikkel would've done?

Oh well. It was another thing that Bree could tick off the list.

Bev checked her iPad. 'Just to confirm then, Portia. We're going with a bottom tier of traditional fruit cake, marzipan, Royal icing and piped decorative edges. Tier two is Madeira cake infused with lavender, iced with a flat white Royal icing, decorated liberally with viola petals. Tier three is a Battenburg, topped with almond-white marzipan and skimmed with icing, decorated with nasturtiums. Tier four is my chocolate cake, covered with a mixture of my chocolate fudge icing and white chocolate and vanilla, decorated with milk, dark and white chocolate shavings and chocolate curls in the shape of trumpets. Tier five is a seahorse crafted from white chocolate, pulling a dark chocolate carriage in which the milk chocolate figures of you and Mikkel will stand. Yes?'

Portia nodded. 'Yes.'

'What could possibly go wrong with that?' Ella asked.

Her sarcasm wasn't lost on Bree who merely shook her head and sighed quietly while Bethany laughed, Mia's mouth fell open and Bev simply smiled.

Portia looked lost in a world of her own and the smile on her face was as close to euphoric as it was possible to get.

'We'll cut each tier individually to avoid one cake intermixing with another,' Portia added after a moment or two. 'Not everyone loves chocolate, or Battenburg, for example, which Mikkel says is his dad's favourite. This way there'll be something that everyone likes.'

If Bev could pull that off, the woman would top Bree's list of bakers for all future weddings. Even if that did mean Jenny Lake might be upset.

Not that Jenny needed to know.

Sometimes it was good to keep a secret.

But sometimes it wasn't.

Especially when you weren't entirely sure what the secret was you were going to have to keep.

Which is exactly what went through Bree's mind less than fifteen minutes later as she, Mia and Ella returned to the hotel.

Twelve

'I would say that was a bit of a waste of time,' Mia said, as she waddled towards the lifts in the vast and rather grand, hotel foyer, 'but I'm happy with any excuse to eat cake.'

Walking was clearly becoming increasingly difficult for her due to her size, and that was before she'd eaten an inordinate amount of Bev's cake samples.

Ella laughed. 'Portia had made up her mind before we arrived. I'm convinced of that. And she had the nerve to say Mikkel was too easily pleased, or words to that effect. Still, as you say, any excuse to eat cake is good. I can't wait to see the finished article. The whole thing sounds a bit bizarre to me, and five tiers of different cakes is a recipe for disaster in my book. Let's hope it doesn't end up like the Leaning Tower of Pisa.'

'I'm sure it'll be fine.' Bree wasn't sure of anything of the sort. She'd tried to sway Portia towards a more refined-looking cake but as Ella had stated, Portia had clearly made up her mind.

But Portia had also said that she and Mikkel had agreed about what they wanted and the number of layers so at least they were in that together.

She glanced towards the bar to their left and for the first time in a very long while, she wished she could have a glass of wine. It had been an extremely long day and although the rain had held off for most of the afternoon, since they'd left Beach Bakers it had become somewhat humid. Getting soaked to the skin, twice, hadn't helped. She really must learn not to listen to Ella.

'God, I could murder a glass of chilled white wine,' Ella said, as if reading Bree's mind.

'Me too,' added Mia. 'Sometimes being pregnant really sucks. Especially in weather like this. I could spend hours lounging in a luxurious bath but the way I feel right now, I probably wouldn't be able to get out. With this belly, I struggle at the best of times.'

'We could ask the hotel if they have a hoist,' Ella suggested. 'Or a crane.'

'Funny.' Mia sneered at her.

'You could go for a swim,' Bree said.

'That's not a bad idea. Except I'm exhausted. Carrying another three people around inside me is hard work, you know. And besides, don't they say that you must wait at least an hour to do exercise of any sort after you've eaten? We've eaten a lot of cake, so on second thoughts, maybe that's not such a good idea. I'm going up to my room, turning the air conditioning up full-pelt, and collapsing on my bed until dinner.'

'Same here,' Ella said, with a final lingering glance towards the bar as they passed by. 'Oh look. Isn't that Mikkel?'

Bree and Mia stopped and followed Ella's line of sight to the broad-shouldered man sitting at the bar. He was seated sideways to the bar which meant he had his back to them but his hair and build were identical to Mikkel's, as were the jeans and T-shirt the man was wearing. That was exactly what Mikkel had on when he'd left them to go to the post office.

And why shouldn't it be Mikkel? He could've popped in for a drink.

'It is,' Mia agreed. 'Should we go and say hello? Oh wait. Do you think he's waiting for Portia? Perhaps he assumed she'd come back here with us instead of getting a minicab to bring us back.'

'Of course. That's it.' Bree wasn't sure why, but when Ella had spotted him, Bree's tummy had lurched uncomfortably. And not because of her baby. Now she sighed with relief.

'Who's that woman he's with?' Ella asked, peering at the beautiful blonde woman perched on the bar stool a little too close to his and staring directly at him. 'It looks as if they're … friends.'

Bree glanced at Ella and Mia and they were obviously thinking the same thing she was as the woman leaned closer.

The blonde woman, who definitely was not Mikkel's fiancée, Portia, in spite of the similar colouring of their hair, was about to kiss Mikkel.

Bree grabbed her friends by their arms and hastily ushered them away.

'Hold on,' Mia said. 'I want to see that.'

'No, you don't!'

'We do,' Ella said, trying to free herself from Bree's firm grip.

'No! We don't.'

'But that woman was about to kiss Mikkel,' Ella said.

'And that wasn't Portia,' Mia added unnecessarily.

'Which is precisely why we do *not* want to see what is happening.' Bree was adamant.

'Speak for yourself,' Ella said, struggling free. 'God, Bree. Your grip is like a vice. My arm's going to be bruised tomorrow.'

'Don't look, Ella! Please!'

Ella frowned. 'Why not? Don't you want to know if he kissed her back or pushed her away?'

Bree shook her head. 'No. Because I had an uneasy feeling the moment I saw him, and I'm Portia's wedding planner. There is no way on this earth that I want to have to tell my client that I saw her fiancé in a hotel bar kissing another woman.'

Ella shrugged. 'Then don't tell her.'

'What? Are you mad? Of course I'd have to tell her.'

'Er. There is another possible explanation,' Mia said. 'The woman could be his sister, or his cousin, or even a close friend. If we'd waited, we might've seen her just give him a peck on the cheek or something.'

'Seriously?' Ella smirked. 'Did she look as if that was what she was going to do?'

They all shook their heads.

'No,' Mia agreed. 'Even from where we were standing it looked pretty obvious that she was going in for a full-on kiss.'

'And he didn't seem to be moving away, did he?' Bree queried.

'No.' Mia sighed. 'But that doesn't mean he knew what she was about to do. Some men are notoriously bad at reading the signs.'

'You shouldn't have dragged us away,' Ella said. 'Now we won't know for certain. Hold on.'

'Ella!' Bree hissed at her but Ella hurried back to their previous vantage point to take a look.

Ella peered into the bar and glanced around before shrugging her shoulders and returning to Bree and Mia.

'They've gone. Vanished. Disappeared.' She furrowed her brows. 'Where could they have gone? Did you see them come out?'

'Nah-uh.' Mia shook her head and scanned the foyer.

'No.' Bree's tummy lurched once more. 'Now where are you going?'

Ella hurried towards the reception desk. 'I'll be back.'

Bree turned to Mia. 'Perhaps I was wrong to drag you away. Maybe we should've stayed and watched what happened. At least then we'd know. We might be barking up the wrong tree entirely and making a mountain out of a molehill.'

'Perhaps. I can't believe Mikkel's cheating on Portia. They looked so in love at lunchtime.'

'They did. It was obvious he adores her. And yet...' Bree couldn't finish her sentence.

Mia did it for her. 'And yet he did seem very keen to come to Easterhill and post those invitations.'

'A bit too keen.'

'And not at all concerned about tasting his own wedding cake.'

'Not in the least. But that doesn't mean he's ... God. I can't bear to even think it, let alone say it.'

Ella, it seemed, had no such qualms as she returned to Bree and Mia.

'He's having an affair. The bastard.'

'What!' Hearing it was still a shock and Bree had to swallow the unpleasant taste of bile. 'How do you know that?'

'Because I asked the receptionist who the woman was. Well, what I said was that I'd just seen a beautiful blonde woman in the bar and I described what she was wearing. I said that it didn't occur to me right away but I thought she looked like an old friend from uni but by the time I realised, the woman had gone, and I wondered if the receptionist knew who she was. The girl beamed at me and said – and wait for this – "That sounds like Mrs Dunn. Diana Dunn. She's a frequent guest of this hotel and she's here today with her husband, the famous cardiac surgeon, Alex Dunn!" Can you bloody believe it?'

'The receptionist shouldn't have given you their details.' Mia was clearly appalled at the breach of confidentiality. 'But at least we now know it wasn't Mikkel.'

'Sod their details,' Ella said, 'and are you mad? Of course it was Mikkel. Apart from the fact that the receptionist went on to say that Mr Dunn would be joining his wife later. Diana Dunn was the woman Portia told us about, remember?' Ella tutted. 'And you say my memory's bad. God. Mikkel's a cheat and a liar.'

'Oh my God!' Mia was now even more appalled, judging by her look of horror.

'But where did they go?' Bree asked.

'Good question,' said Ella. 'I asked the receptionist that. Well, not where they'd gone, but how 'my friend' could've slipped by me without me spotting her again. She said there's a door from the bar leading onto a terrace. A bit like the one we had breakfast on, but this one has steps down to the hotel forecourt. Basically, because the bar's open to the public, not just hotel guests. Anyway, there's also another set of lifts at the other side of the bar. They're mainly for people going to the spa area and can be accessed via the bar or from this side of the foyer. But they also serve the upper floors … where the bedrooms are.'

Ella emphasised that point even though she didn't need to.

Bree frowned. 'What you're saying is that Mikkel either left via the front entrance to the bar ... or he went upstairs with ... Diana.'

'Yep.'

'We could check to see if his car's still here,' Mia suggested.

'Do you know what car he drives?' Ella asked.

'No. But I do recall seeing several cars in his drive at lunch and I might recognise one of them if I saw it again.'

'Seriously?' Ella's look was doubtful.

'I didn't notice the cars,' Bree said. 'I was too busy drooling over the façade of his house.'

'I was admiring the view,' Ella said. 'Especially once we got inside and I saw Mikkel. Why are the gorgeous ones always the cheats and liars?'

'They're not,' Mia said. 'Jet's far more handsome than Mikkel and he's not a cheat or a liar. And Gill and Garrick are gorgeous too and they don't cheat or lie.'

'As far as we know,' Ella mumbled.

'What?' Bree glared at her. 'Are you now suggesting our husbands might be cheating on us? Honestly, Ella. Sometimes you say the most annoying things.'

'I'm not suggesting anything. All I'm saying is it's possible. Especially now when we're like three beached whales and that new barmaid Toby's hired is tall and slim and has boobs that look like ripe peaches, not over inflated beach balls as ours do right now.'

Bree and Mia stared at her, but Bree couldn't argue with that.

Toby Bywater ran their village pub, The Frog and Lily, along with his sister, Alexia and his live-in partner, Christy. Their parents, the owners, had retired to Spain and Alexia, who was married to the village vet, Rupert Day, known to everyone as Bear, had just given birth to a son and was taking maternity leave. So Toby had employed a temporary barmaid. One or two villagers had joked that he'd hired the most beautiful girl he could find, but she was actually the daughter of a friend of Christy's, who wanted to spend a summer by the sea. The fact that the girl was only twenty-one, had the body and looks of a supermodel and was fit, tanned and "up for anything" – her words, gave the rest of the women in Little Pondale a few concerns, however much they trusted their husbands or boyfriends or partners.

'My boobs never looked as good as hers even before I was pregnant,' Mia said, sighing. 'But I trust Jet implicitly.

'Of course you do,' Ella said. 'And he'll never go back to his old ways no matter how much that damn girl flirts with him.'

Mia glowered at her. 'If that was supposed to be reassuring, Ella, I'm not certain it's having the desired effect.'

'It was. Honestly. He's not like Gill. My bloody husband hangs on her every word.'

Mia tutted. 'Only because she's as fascinated in history as he is. That's all they talk about when he goes to the pub. I've heard them. We all have.'

'Yeah. But I sometimes wonder what they talk about if they're not in the pub.'

'Are you saying you've seen them together away from The Frog and Lily? Is that why you've really been behaving so weirdly?' Mia threw a worried glance at Bree. 'Gill adores you, Ella. He would no more have an affair than Jet would.'

'Yeah, yeah. I know. And no. I haven't seen them together outside of the pub. But we're not with our husbands every second of every day, are we? And at present, they're all alone twenty-four-seven. Plus, none of them tried very hard to stop us coming here, did they? Who knows what's going on in Little Pondale right now?'

'I think,' Bree said, anxious to change the subject and not wonder what Garrick might be doing, 'we're getting off the matter in hand. I, for one, am certain Garrick, Jet and Gill are being completely faithful and going about their business as usual. Apart from missing us dreadfully, of course. Unlike Mikkel, who it seems, might not be behaving quite so gallantly. The question is, what do we do now?'

'I'm going to call Jet and tell him how much I love him and that if he ever dares to think about cheating on me, he's dead.' Mia waddled towards the lift.

'I'm not phoning Gill,' Ella said. 'I'm hoping Hettie will be keeping an eye on everyone in the village, as per usual. She'll call me if that barmaid comes within an inch of our cottage.'

'Garrick's far too busy with our kids to have time for an affair,' Bree said. 'Even if he wanted to. And I don't think he does. God, Ella. Why did you have to mention that?'

Ella shrugged. 'I'm tired. I'm hot. And I could murder a glass of wine which I'm not allowed to have. I'm not in the best of moods. So sue me.'

'I'm tempted to beat you around the head,' Mia said.

'Me too,' said Bree, as they stepped into the lift. 'But that still doesn't solve the problem with Mikkel and Diana. What are we going to say to Portia?'

Thirteen

'I don't think we should say anything to Portia,' Ella said as she, Bree and Mia sat down to dinner in the hotel restaurant that evening.

'Why the change of tune?' Bree asked. She was much happier now, having spoken at length with Garrick shortly after going to her room.

Ella shrugged. 'Because Gill called me just now and we had a long chat. I told him about what we'd seen and he gave me a lecture on jumping to conclusions.' She lowered her gaze and sighed. 'And then, when I said that sometimes people made it hard not to jump to conclusions, and I happened to mention the new barmaid in The Frog and Lily, I got an even longer lecture. In fact, he got quite cross. He told me I needed to find something to occupy my mind so that it didn't keep running off into fantasy land. He reminded me that he was the one who writes fiction and I was the serious, no nonsense editor. Or I used to be. He also said he understands what I'm going through but that having doubts about his loyalty to me is ludicrous and my fears are totally unfounded. But then he would say that, wouldn't he?'

'Oh for heaven's sake, Ella, will you stop!' Mia slapped her on the arm. 'You even had me doubting Jet. And that's something I haven't done since we had that slight misunderstanding before we got married. But I realised how silly I was being the moment he called me this evening. And I never want to hear you questioning our husbands' faithfulness again, okay? Jet adores me. Garrick adores Bree. And Gill adores you. End of story. Now let's concentrate on Portia and Mikkel. Why don't you think we should tell her? Because we may have misinterpreted what we think we saw? Is that it?'

Ella was suitably chastised and her smile was apologetic. 'Yeah. And you're right. I'm sorry. And Gill did say he adores me. After the lecture, that is. And that, no matter how beautiful I might think the new barmaid is, in his eyes, she's a plain Jane compared to me.' Her smile broadened. 'Why do we get ourselves so worked up about these things? God. I'm starving. What's on the menu tonight?'

She took the leather-bound menu from the waiter who had arrived at the table, and they listened intently as he reeled off an impressive list of 'specials' in addition to those written on the menus he'd given each of them.

Bree decided on the plaice poached in saffron and cream, and returned the menu to the waiter. Once Ella had selected the same and Mia had chosen the pan-seared tuna, Bree leant forward and looked around to check she couldn't be overheard.

'I also told Garrick and he said the same as Gill. That we might have misconstrued the situation.'

'Jet did too,' Mia said. 'He said we should give the guy the benefit of the doubt. But he added that if we feel we need to talk to anyone about what we think we saw, it should be Mikkel, not Portia. And he reminded me of our little misunderstanding and how that situation could've escalated into something it never was.'

'You think we should ask Mikkel about it?' Bree wasn't convinced.

'No. I'm saying that Jet says if we feel we need to, we should. But do we need to? That's my question. We could simply mention that we saw him in the hotel bar and see what he says, couldn't we?'

'Only not when Portia's in earshot,' Ella said. 'She might overhear us and ... jump to conclusions.'

'Like you would?' Mia grinned, in spite of the seriousness of the situation.

Ella nodded. 'Like I would.'

'That's what we'll do then.' Bree made a decision. 'We'll wait until we can get Mikkel alone and we'll say that as casually as we can.'

'She was drop-dead gorgeous though, wasn't she?' Ella said, a moment or so later as she glanced around the room. 'Diana, I mean. Portia's gorgeous too, but there was something about Diana. Even from several feet away, she looked like she belonged on the cover of a posh magazine, like Vogue, or something and – oh dear God. Look! She's here. Having dinner. And that's definitely not Mikkel.'

'That must be her husband,' Mia said, staring at the couple seated at a table at the other end of the room.

'Wow!' Bree said, leaning to one side to get a better view while trying not to fall from her chair. 'He must be the heart surgeon.'

'Heart throb, more like,' Ella said. 'Why would she want Mikkel when her husband looks like that? Although Mikkel's handsome too, but my God, that man is something else.'

'The heart wants what the heart wants,' Bree said.

'Perhaps Diana's heart wants both,' said Mia. 'I know what that feels like.' She darted a look at Bree, gave a brief apologetic smile, and quickly looked away.

'You mean when you loved both Garrick and Jet,' Bree said, without a hint of jealousy or resentment.

She knew all about the history between Garrick, Jet and Mia, as did everyone else who lived in Little Pondale. But it was exactly that. History. Destiny had carved out their paths and, as Garrick had said, once or twice, "Everything turned out the way it was meant to be, even if some hearts did take a bit of a beating along the way".

Perhaps that would happen here.

Perhaps Destiny had carved out Portia, Mikkel and Diana's paths and all that was left was to see which path led where.

Destiny had led Bree to Little Pondale and to Garrick. And there was nowhere else on earth she'd rather be.

Not even in Seahorse Harbour, planning Portia Trulove's wedding.

Fourteen

'I don't understand,' Portia said. 'Have I done something wrong? Was it something I said?'

Bree let out a pent-up sigh and shook her head. She'd been dreading this since dinner last night, when she realised just how much she was missing Garrick and the kids. And when she'd woken up this morning still feeling exactly the same, she had made a decision. She'd mentioned it to Mia and Ella over breakfast and they'd both thought she was mad. Although they admitted to feeling the same.

'Absolutely not. It's not about you. It's about me. I wanted to say yes to planning your wedding because, well, having Portia Trulove on my list of clients was a massive coup for me. But you don't need a wedding planner, Portia. You'd done a brilliant job before we arrived and you'll do a brilliant job if we leave. You know exactly what you want. You have as many, if not more, contacts as me. And I'm not saying I won't assist you in any way I can. But I can do that from my home in Little Pondale. You don't need me here. Or Mia and Ella. And the truth is, I'm missing my husband much more than I thought I would. And my kids.'

'Oh.' Portia looked deflated. Like bright confetti that had once danced and swirled in the air but had now fallen to the ground and been left to fade. 'Well, if that's what you want then there's nothing much I can say, is there?' She brightened briefly. 'Your husband and kids could come here. I mean to Easterhill. To the hotel. My treat. And Mia and Ella's husbands could come too. Would that make a difference? Would you stay?'

'My husband has a bespoke furniture business to run and orders to fulfil. Mia's husband owns a farm. Gill could come. He's a writer and could do that anywhere. But that's not the issue. The point is, you don't need us, Portia. You don't need a wedding planner. It's all as good as done. I'm happy to keep an eye on everything, from a distance, to make certain nothing slips through the net, and I'm more than happy to be here on the wedding day to ensure it all runs smoothly, if you like. But we're just wasting your time and money by staying at the hotel. As wonderful as it is.'

'You want to go home. I get that. And I completely understand. But please don't give up your role. I do need a wedding planner, whatever you might think.' Portia sighed. 'Okay. I'll admit that's probably not true. I don't need one. I want one. I've been decisive all my life. I've always known what I wanted and how to get it. I'm a brilliant negotiator, even if I say so myself. But this is all new territory for me. Since I met Mikkel, my life, my world, has turned upside down. Marriage and kids weren't that important to me. Now being married to Mikkel and starting a family with him is the most important thing in my life. Nothing else matters. Not even the luxury eco hotel we're going to build.' She gave a little laugh. 'What I'm trying to say is that just having you and Mia and Ella here is helping to make this all feel real. Does that make sense? Sometimes I think this is all just a wonderful dream and that it's not reality. Having a wedding planner makes me realise it is. Okay. That sounds crazy even to me.'

'No. I understand that. I never thought I'd get married. And definitely not to Garrick. I'd loved him since I was a child but we'd lost touch. Seeing him again was like a miracle, and when he told me he loved me, I felt it must be a dream and that one day I'd wake up and discover it was.'

'That's how I feel. I think I might wake up and discover Mikkel doesn't love me, after all. Wait. Is there something you're not telling me, Bree? I just saw a look on your face when I said that, and I'm not sure what to make of it. Are you ... are you thinking this is all happening way too fast and that either me, or more likely Mikkel, will have second thoughts and call the whole thing off?'

'No.' Bree cleared her throat. 'No. It's nothing like that.'

'Bree?' Portia coaxed. 'What is it?'

'I told you what it was. You don't need us. And we ... we're all missing our husbands.'

'Bree. Please don't lie to me. I'm sure you're telling the truth about missing your husbands. I missed Mikkel dreadfully when I went to see my dad and Bethany. But there's more to this, isn't there? Has something happened? Has someone said or done something? Oh God. This isn't about Diana, is it? She ... she hasn't threatened you or anything like that. God! What am I saying? As if she'd do that. Hold on though. Why did you react like that when I mentioned her name?'

'Like what? I didn't react.'

'Yes, you did. Like she was a ghost at my party. Is this ... about Diana in some way?'

'Hello, Bree.' Mikkel strolled into his sitting room, beaming at Bree as if he were genuinely pleased to see her but his face changed almost immediately and the smile slid from his lips. 'What's wrong? What's happened?'

'That's what I'm trying to find out,' Portia said, her tone calm and controlled, if somewhat cooler than it had been yesterday, towards her fiancé. 'But I believe it may have something to do with Diana.'

Mikkel's face contorted into a picture of guilt as his concerned stare darted from Portia to Bree and back again. His Adam's apple rose and fell and he swallowed hard as he clearly struggled to force out his words.

'Diana? What ... what could have possibly happened with Diana to produce that look on your face?'

Fifteen

Everything happened so fast.

One minute, Bree was trying to explain to Portia why she felt she, Mia and Ella should go home to Little Pondale. The next, she was assuring Portia they would stay in the hotel at Easterhill for as long as Portia wanted, and the next, she was in the back of a minicab, returning to the Easterhill Hotel and Spa.

A few minutes later, she was sitting in the bar, drinking coffee with her friends and watching rivers of rainwater cascading down the floor to ceiling windows overlooking the terrace.

'Let me get this straight,' Ella said, lounging back in a sumptuous dark green leather chair, her blonde curls resting on her shoulders, and a look of disbelief written all over her face. 'You got a cab to Mikkel's this morning, without discussing it with Mia and me, to tell Portia we were leaving, and you end up spilling the beans on Mikkel and Diana.'

'No. Er ... yes. Um. Not exactly.'

'Which is it?' Mia demanded.

Bree fiddled with the buttons on the front of her dress.

'Portia sensed something was wrong and Mikkel appeared at that precise moment. It was Portia who mentioned Diana. Not me. But Mikkel looked as guilty as sin, believe me. And then I let it slip – don't ask me why or how. It just sort of came out. I ... I said that the three of us saw him in the bar. This bar.'

Ella tutted. 'We know where he was. What did he say?'

'Um. He said, "And?" Just like that. So ... I didn't say anything else. I just stood there. Portia looked at me and then at him and back to me and said that it was clear there was more to be said.'

'He said, "I think what Bree may be trying to tell you is that she saw me and someone else in the bar at the Easterhill Hotel. Is that it, Bree? What a shame. I didn't have you down as a gossip."'

'A gossip?' Mia fumed. 'He called you a gossip? What a cheek!'

'What happened next?' Ella asked, not even trying to hide the excitement on her face.

'I reacted as Mia just did. And I assured him I didn't gossip.'

'Then what?'

'Portia asked him who he was with and he replied, "I wasn't with anyone."'.

'The liar!' Mia said.

Bree nodded. 'I could see he was worried though. It was evident in his eyes and also in the way he was standing. He looked just like a Viking warrior defending his kingdom – although without the shining armour.'

'Vikings didn't wear shining armour,' Ella said. 'That was our lot.'

'For someone whose husband writes both factual and fictional books and novels, mainly based in the past, your grasp of history is appalling,' Mia said. 'Vikings had armour too.'

'I didn't say they didn't. I said it wasn't shining.'

'Shut up you two,' Bree snapped. 'No one cares about Vikings.'

'I think you'll find several people do.' Ella grinned. 'But okay. Not in this context. What happened next?'

Bree let out an exasperated sigh.

'Portia looked at me in a sort of bemused way as if asking me to explain but I didn't want to say anything, because then I would've been gossiping. But I didn't need to say a word, because Mikkel did.'

'What did he say?' Ella sat upright now, eager to hear more.

'He said, "I went to the hotel because there was something I needed to do. I'd rather not elaborate because that will spoil something I was doing for someone else. I popped into the bar for a pint and ... Diana appeared from nowhere." Portia didn't look pleased.'

'I bet she didn't.'

'Honestly, Ella. You really shouldn't smile about it.'

'I'm not smiling. I'm sneering. There's a big difference.'

Mia tutted. 'What did Portia say?'

'She said, "Diana! I knew it." And she looked really upset. Then Mikkel said, "Now before you start putting two and two together and making sixteen, please give me a chance to tell you what happened." He tried to take her hand but she backed away.'

'Good for her,' said Ella.

Bree shook her head. Portia said, "Fine." Even though it clearly wasn't fine at all. And Mikkel looked at me and said, "I'd rather do it in private. Bree? I'm calling a cab to take you back to the hotel. We'll be in touch once we've … discussed this matter." I just nodded because I didn't know what to say.'

'So you left?' Ella seemed surprised and disappointed.

'Not right away, no. Portia asked, "Why don't you want Bree to stay?" and Mikkel replied, "Because this isn't just about us. This is about Diana too. And there's been enough gossip about her recently. I don't want more flying around. And it also involves others." Portia was furious. "So you're trying to protect Diana?", she said. I thought she was going to throw something at him.'

'I would have,' Ella said.

'Yes. I expect you would. But Portia didn't. She just stood there with her chin stuck out, glowering at him, and he said, "No. I'm trying to prevent more people getting hurt due to speculation, gossip and others not minding their own business." To which Portia replied, "I want Bree to stay." I felt as if I were being torn in two.'

'And then?' Mia coaxed.

Bree shrugged. Then Mikkel said, "Then we'll have to discuss this another time, because as much as I love you. And I love you more than almost anything, Portia. I am not discussing this in front of Bree."'

'Wow,' Ella said. 'He really is a Viking, isn't he?'

Bree tutted. 'He called a cab and the three of us just stood there for a moment and then Portia said, "Okay" and she asked me if I'd mind leaving them. She said she'd call me later and she even came outside to make sure I got in the cab safely because she said she was worried this had upset me. Upset me! The poor woman must have been going mad. She did ask me if I would tell her what I saw but I told her that I didn't really know if I saw anything and besides, Mikkel was right. This was none of my business and I didn't want to gossip. We stood in almost unbearable silence and waited the few minutes until the cab arrived. I could see she was chomping at the bit to get back inside but I also think she was taking the time to think and to calm herself down. Anyway. That's it. The cab came, we drove away and Portia went back inside.'

'Bloody Nora,' Ella said, fighting the grin that clearly tugged at her mouth. 'Who knew planning a wedding could be this exciting? Shall we make a bet on whether it's on or off?'

'No, Ella!' Bree and Mia said in unison.

'Portia will be heartbroken if Mikkel did kiss Diana,' Bree said.

'Unless we got it wrong.' Mia looked thoughtful. 'I know you said he looked guilty, but he didn't immediately make an excuse, did he? In fact, the way he reacted, from what you've said, almost makes it sound as if he didn't know Diana was at the hotel. Until she turned up in the bar.'

'What?' Ella threw her a doubtful look. 'You mean he popped in for a drink and she just happened to be here too?'

'No. She was here. Waiting for her husband. The receptionist said he was arriving later, didn't she? And we saw him ourselves, so we know that's true. What if Mikkel did just come for a drink and when Diana saw him, she went to say hello?'

'Aren't you forgetting one thing?' Ella asked. 'The kiss.'

'Hmmm. But we didn't see them kiss, did we? Perhaps she went to kiss him and he pushed her away?'

Bree nodded. 'That's possible.'

'And again,' Mia said. 'I can speak from experience about people misinterpreting a kiss. And who kissed whom and stuff. It's not always as straightforward as it appears.'

'Then we have to hope that's what happened, don't we?' Bree said. 'And that Portia and Mikkel can talk it through.'

Ella was uncharacteristically silent for a moment, but it didn't last long.

'Does this mean we're going home, or staying here? Only if we're going home, I want to see if I can have one more treatment in the spa before we leave.'

'Ella Swan! I mean, De Fonteneau. You are unbelievable sometimes.'

'What? I feel sorry for her, Bree. I really do. But us worrying about it won't make any difference, will it? What will be, will be. And how often do we get to spend time in the spa of a luxury hotel? I'm sorry if you think I'm being callous, but I can feel just as much sympathy for Portia while being pampered in the spa, as I can sitting here and drinking coffee. And frankly, I know which of those I'd rather be doing.'

Sixteen

Josie buried her head in her hands for a moment before staring at her sister who sat on the sofa diagonally opposite her.

'Say something then,' Diana commanded. 'You know you want to.'

Josie shook her head. 'I don't know what to say. How could you do it? And more importantly, why?'

Diana laughed although it morphed into a part maniacal scream, part strangled sob.

'I don't know, Josie. Honestly, I don't. I was feeling happier than I had in days. You know I was. When I asked you to look after Henry, you even commented on that.'

'I did. And you did look happier. So what went wrong?'

Diana let out a short and rather angry sigh. She uncurled herself from the semi-foetal position she'd adopted the second she sat on Josie and Liam's sofa, and banged her mug on the coffee table in front of her.

'Everything. No. Not everything. I'd told myself I wasn't going to think about Mikkel, and then there he was, sitting at the hotel bar. I saw him as I was waiting for the lift to take me back to the room, and my resolve melted faster than the eyebrow wax I'd just had.'

'So you went over and tried to kiss him? And that seemed like a good idea?'

'No. I went over to say hello. I apologised for Friday night and told him I was meeting Alex and we were having dinner at the hotel and spending the night. I asked what he was doing there and he said he'd just popped in for a drink because he had some business at the hotel.'

'What business?'

'He didn't say and I didn't ask.'

'And then you tried to kiss him?'

'Yes. No. Not right away. As I just told you. One minute we were chatting. It was awkward at first and then we both relaxed into a semi-normal conversation, and the next minute I had an overwhelming urge to kiss him. I don't know what came over me. Everything was going well until I leant forward and planted a kiss on his mouth.'

'And he backed away and held you off?'

Diana nodded. 'It took him a second or two to realise what was happening and he nearly fell off his chair. After I made a complete fool of myself, I dashed to my room and tried to drown myself in the shower. Not literally, before you have me certified and dragged off to some asylum. I wept my heart out. I don't know how long I spent in there but when I eventually came out, I felt ... lighter, somehow. I tried to call Mikkel to apologise but he wouldn't take my call. I ... I did actually consider – for just a second, or maybe less. A split second. How much better it might be for everyone if I wasn't around to mess things up.'

'Diana! Dear God. Are you serious?'

'Don't panic. I told you it was a fleeting thought. I wouldn't have done anything. I might've got exceedingly drunk though. But Becca called. Right at that very moment, and she told me that Noah's coming home with her this weekend and they've got something wonderful to tell us.'

'Oh God. Please don't tell me she's getting engaged. I couldn't bear it if my niece got married before me. Sorry. I don't know where that came from. Carry on.'

Diana frowned at her. 'She'd better not be getting engaged. I love Noah but Becca's far too young for that.'

'Er. You weren't that much older, I seem to recall.'

'Okay. But that was different. Anyway, she did say I wasn't to worry and that she definitely wasn't going to tell us she's pregnant or anything, so that's a relief. And as she chatted away it was as if I had some sort of epiphany. Don't give me that look. I did. I sat there and thought how stupid and selfish and ridiculous I'd been. You're always telling me how lucky I am and I know that's true. But for the first time in ages I felt truly blessed and grateful and lucky and ... loved. And then a little later, Alex arrived and he smiled at me in a way I haven't seen him smile for a long time, and I realised I do still love him. I knew I did. But I didn't think I loved him enough to spend the rest of my life with him.' She swung her legs back beneath her but this time she sat up and smiled as she spoke. 'Oh Josie. We had such a wonderful evening. A really fantastic time. We even had sex like we used to.'

'Too much information, thanks.' Josie pulled a face but she smiled at her sister.

'Sorry. But you know what I mean. Passionate, rampant, crazy sex. And we laughed and we drank champagne and we made love in the shower and ... and we did things we hadn't done for a long time. And then I was overcome with guilt, so this morning, I blurted out that I had tried to kiss Mikkel in the bar yesterday. And how awful I'd felt afterwards and then how I'd had my ... revelation. Do you know what Alex said?'

'Oh Hell. No. Tell me.'

'He said, "That wouldn't have happened if you'd come here with Josie or Elsie or Lottie, as I'd suggested. But that was yesterday afternoon. Last night made up for that and if you promise me it will never happen again, I think we can get over it. You've forgiven me for far more than that." And that's true. I have.' She took a deep breath. 'So we're trying to work things out. We're giving our marriage another shot. A real one this time. And we're going to continue with counselling and we're going to spend a lot more time together. I'm ... I'm even going back to our Blackheath house for the odd night every so often. I don't want to spend too many days on my own while Alex works though, so it'll only be on the days he's got a short list of procedures, or he's only doing a few consultations.'

'And ... Mikkel?'

Diana closed her eyes and her sigh was long and wistful but her mouth curved into a smile.

'I love him. There's no denying that. But he's marrying ... Portia and that's the end of that. I'm determined to get over him. I must. So that's it. What do you think?'

Josie hesitated. 'About what? You and Alex? Or you getting over Mikkel?'

'Both. All of it. Everything.'

Josie reached out and took Diana's hand. 'I think all this is the best news I've heard in weeks. I'm proud of you, Diana. You can do this. Alex has changed beyond all recognition and I really believe you two could have a bright future. I never thought I'd be singing Alex's praises but he's turned himself around. I'm sure of it. If he can do it, it'll be a breeze for you. But may I give you a few words of advice?'

'Of course.'

'Stay away from Mikkel. And from Portia. And if you ever get the urge to kiss Mikkel again, run in the other direction as fast as you can and give me a call instead. Okay?'

Diana sucked in a breath, gave Josie a smile, and nodded. 'Agreed.'

'Great. Let's drink to that. I'm so happy for you, Di. I really am.'

Josie jumped up from her seat and hurried to the kitchen returning a minute later with champagne and two glasses and stepping over Henry who was fast asleep on her sitting room floor. Diana was stroking

161

him and his eyelids flickered slightly in his sleep.

'I am exceedingly lucky, aren't I?' Diana said, taking the glass of bubbly Josie handed her. 'I've got a loving husband and two wonderful kids. I've even got the greatest dog in the world.' She smiled at Josie. 'And I've definitely got the best sister any woman could ask for. I love you, Josie. I really do.'

'And I love you. Cheers to us,' Josie said, as they clinked glasses. 'Now if only I could find a way to get Liam to propose, our happiness would be truly complete.'

Sixteen

Portia glared at Mikkel. 'Explain then.'

He dragged a hand through his hair and met her stare.

'Do you honestly believe that I had arranged to meet Diana? Just tell me that.'

'I ... I don't know. I don't think so – but you might've done. Only ... I can't believe you would. Not really. Unless she begged you to and you felt you had to. Or she threatened to do something and you wanted to try to stop her. Is that what happened?'

'You don't believe I was in the bar and she came in and it was just a coincidence?'

Portia shrugged. 'I suppose it could've been. But why were you there? And why was she?'

'She was there because her husband had paid for her to spend a day at the spa and he was meeting her there for dinner later. At least that's what she told me when she came over to say hello.'

'To say hello?'

'Yes. I admit I was concerned but she seemed fine and in control. She sat down and we chatted. She told me about Alex. She even asked how things were going with the wedding. And then out of nowhere, she suddenly leant forward and tried to kiss me. I held her away as soon as it dawned on me what she was doing. I told her not to make things awkward for either of us and she apologised and turned and raced away. I'll admit it was a bit of a shock, so I finished my drink and left. That's it. Do you believe me?'

She studied his face. 'Yes. I think so.'

'You think so? Or you do?'

'I do. But why were you there? You haven't said.'

'Because it's a surprise for a friend and I don't want to spoil it. You either trust me or you don't. I adore you, Portia, but I've told you it's over with Diana and it is. I can promise you I will never, ever, cheat on you with Diana. Or with anyone, in fact. But what I can't – and won't, promise you, is to never speak to her or be seen in the same place when she just happens to be there. It's a tiny village and we all live here. I can't spend my future worrying that you won't trust me whenever I bump into Diana.'

'I trust you, Mikkel. I do. It's Diana I'm not so thrilled about.'

'But she can't force me to do something I don't want to do. I care about her. She's still someone I consider a friend. No longer a close friend, but a friend. She's going through a tough time at the moment, and I accept she's doing some crazy things, but she'll get through it. I'm sure of that. I'm not going to ignore her, Portia. That would be petty, rude and frankly, unnecessary. I will try to stay out of her way though. Okay?'

'Okay. I suppose. Yes, okay. I understand. You promise to try to avoid her and I'll promise to try not to get jealous, or concerned or to have any doubts about you. About us. I'm sorry. I should've trusted you. I should've known you wouldn't do something like that behind my back. It won't happen again. But, in future, if you do bump into Diana, please tell me about it as soon as you can. That way I won't get any surprises.'

He nodded as he reached out and gently pulled her into his arms.

'Okay. I'll do that. But let me make this abundantly clear, once and for all. You're the only woman I ever want to kiss, or have wanted to kiss since the day we met. The only woman I want to be with. I love you with all my heart, Portia and I can't wait to be your husband.'

'I love you too, Mikkel. And I can't wait to be your wife. Oh flipping heck! I'd better call Bree. And just so that you know, she didn't tell me anything. She didn't gossip. I guessed there was something wrong and I guessed it was about Diana.'

She turned to look for her phone but Mikkel eased her back to him.

'Bree can wait. Although I clearly owe her an apology. Let's go upstairs and ... talk about our wedding.'

Portia could see in his eyes that talking wasn't what he had in mind.

She smiled up at him and her heart was filled with love for this man whom she knew loved her more than she could ever wish for, but who was also loyal to his friends, even if they didn't deserve that loyalty, and even if, in spite of what she'd said, she couldn't help but worry just a little. It wasn't that she didn't trust him. She did. It was Diana she didn't trust.

'Okay,' she said, as he moved closer to kiss her. 'I'm more than happy to talk about our wedding.'

But talking wasn't what she had in mind either.

Seventeen

'We're staying,' Bree said, after finishing the call from Portia and smiling at Mia and Ella. 'But only for another day. Portia's agreed that we can handle everything else from home. We'll come back for the weekend of the wedding, from Thursday night till Sunday morning. Garrick, Jet and Gill are invited to the wedding too, so we'll have to work something out with our kids, although Portia did just say they're welcome.' She pulled a face. 'But babies at a wedding is a definite no, as far as I'm concerned.'

'Does that mean we're leaving tomorrow or the day after?' Ella queried. 'Is the "another day" today or tomorrow?'

Bree frowned. 'It's tomorrow. The "another day", that is. We're staying today and tomorrow and leaving the day after.'

'Excellent,' Ella said. 'That means I should be able to book in another couple of treatments before we go.'

'And we'll get to see more of Seahorse Harbour,' Mia said. 'I spotted the water spout thingy they call The Weeping Eye yesterday as our cab drove along the cliffs. I'd like to get a closer look at that. When the tide comes in, especially when the sea is rough, water pours into the cave in the inlet near a place called The Shallows and, due to the angles of the rocks and the pressure build-up inside, water is forced upwards and a jet of water spurts out from a hole on the top of the cliffs. That's The Weeping Eye. It's a popular, tourist attraction.'

'I read about that,' Bree said. 'You can take a hot air balloon flight, or go in one of the sightseeing planes from the nearby air club right here in Easterhill, and fly over Seahorse Harbour. The seahorse shape of the bay is more noticeable from the air and The Weeping Eye really does look like an eye. Apparently, you can see the edges and sides of the cliff, like an iris, leading down towards a shimmering blue pool below, which you can swim in when the tide is out. Although only with a local or one of a group of volunteers called The Seahorse Riders. They're the guys who look after the seahorses. When the tide comes in, the pool's like a swirling vortex, so the brochure said.'

'You're not getting me in a hot air balloon or a tiny plane,' Ella said. 'Not that we could fit in either at the moment. I would like to see the water spout thing though. Oh, and the seahorses. You can see them in the sea life centre called Seahorse Tales. That's just along the promenade from Seahorse Bites Café. We could do that today, couldn't we? The weather doesn't look bad.'

'Unless Portia wants us to do anything for her wedding,' Bree pointed out. 'That is why we're here, after all. Not to have spa treatments and visit tourist attractions.'

Ella stuck out her tongue. 'Spoil sport.'

Bree laughed. 'That's very mature.'

'Does she?' Mia asked. 'Want us to do anything for her wedding, today?'

'Er. She didn't say so. No. She did say Mikkel wants to apologise for what he said to me and she suggested we meet for lunch at 1.00 at The Seahorse Inn.'

Ella glanced at her watch. 'It's 11.30 now so that doesn't leave us much time. We could get a cab and pop into the sea life centre. That's only a short walk from the pub and as it's not very big it won't take long to have a look around. I only want to see the seahorses.'

'That sounds like a good plan. Let's do that.'

They grabbed their things and less than twenty minutes later they were standing in Seahorse Tales, admiring a shimmering pool of seahorses seemingly dancing among the sea grasses.

'They're beautiful,' Ella said. 'I knew they would be but they're even better in real life.'

'They're magical, aren't they?' Bree said with a soft sigh.

'They're ...' Mia's voice trailed off.

'They're what?' Ella asked, staring at Mia. 'Why are you looking so surprised? Aren't they like you expected?'

Mia slowly shook her head, as an odd sort of grin spread across her face.

'Funny you should mention "expected". Well, maybe not funny, exactly. Er. Oh my God. I think we need to call Jet, Ella. Right now, please. Unless I'm very much mistaken, I think I'm going to have our babies!'

Eighteen

Jet made it to the hospital in time to witness the birth of their babies in spite of traffic jams, a sudden downpour, and Ella giving him the wrong directions.

Fortunately, Gill was with him when Ella had called and had managed to decipher her manic shrieks and garbled sentences when Jet handed him the phone in total confusion.

'I can't understand what she's saying,' Jet said. 'They're with the seahorses but there's a guy called Asher there who rides them and he's a volunteer vet or something.'

'Ella?' Gill said, calmly. 'Slow down and explain. I'm putting you on speaker. Is everything okay? You sound very excited. What's this about people riding seahorses? Do you want us to come and see something? Or ... Ella? Has something happened? Just say yes or no. Is Mia having her babies?'

'What!' Jet yelped.

'Yes!' shrieked Ella. 'That's what I've been telling you!'

Gill shot a look at Jet. 'We need to go.'

Jet was already racing to his car.

Gill continued talking to Ella as they clambered into it.

'What's happening? Where are you? At the hotel?'

'I don't know what's happening. And no. We're not at the hotel.' Ella sounded as if she were in a total state of shock.

'No? Then where are you?'

Mia screamed at the top of her lungs and Jet almost crashed his car.

'I am not having my babies in a sea life centre,' Mia screeched as Jet and Gill exchanged anxious glances.

'He's a vet,' said Ella, sounding as anxious as Jet felt. 'You'd let Bear deliver your babies and he's a vet.'

'Mia,' a man's voice said. 'I'm Asher and I'm a friend of Mikkel's. Your waters have broken and your babies are coming. I've called an ambulance and it's on the way but there's nothing you can do to stop this if they decide to come right now. Although I believe that's unusual with triplets, and that's what Bree here has said you're expecting, so I'm sure we've got plenty of time. Just breathe and keep calm. I'm here and I know what to do until the ambulance arrives.'

'Mia!' Jet shouted. 'I'm coming. Are you okay?'

'No, I'm not!' She let out a scream. 'I mean, yes. I'm fine. Owwwww! Don't worry about me. Oh my God! Jet! Drive safely. Just get here!'

'She sounds as if she's dying.' Jet almost sobbed the words.

'She's having contractions,' Gill said. 'They hurt a lot sometimes, apparently. Try not to kill us, please.'

Jet was breaking every speed limit, not that he cared about that. He needed to get to Mia and that was all he could think about.

'Asher?' Gill shouted above Mia's screams. 'Where are you?'

Asher gave directions to the sea life centre and also to the hospital.

'I'll let you know when the ambulance arrives,' Asher said, 'so stay on the line. If you get cut off, we'll call you back. I'm a vet but I know what to do so try not to panic. We're slowly making our way to the exit to meet the ambulance. Mia is fine and everything seems normal.'

'Normal?' Mia shrieked. 'There's nothing normal about this.'

'At least they've got rid of the other tourists,' Ella said.

173

'Tourists?' Jet queried, darting a look at Gill.

Gill shrugged. 'Well, it is a sea life centre. I suppose there would be tourists. What's going on now? It's gone a bit quiet.'

'It's all fine,' Asher said. 'Mia's stopped for a moment, that's all.'

'I'm not giving birth here,' Mia said, as if through gritted teeth. 'I am *not*. Where's that bloody ambulance?'

'I can hear the sirens,' Bree said, and so could Jet over the speaker phone. 'It's here, Mia. The ambulance is here.'

'Thank God for that,' Ella said. 'Gill? We'll see you at the hospital. I've checked on my phone and there's a short cut.'

Which there was – only not to the right hospital.

Thankfully, Asher realised Ella's mistake and gave Gill the right directions. None of them trusted any other form of navigation at that moment. Jet and Gill had been sent down too many wrong turns by the satellite navigation not working quite as well as it should in the depths of the countryside around Little Pondale and beyond.

Jet drove like a man whose life depended on it. He was terrified for Mia, but ecstatic at the thought that at any moment he would be a dad.

Once Mia was in the ambulance, he had no idea what was happening and that was even more worrying than hearing his beloved wife screaming at the top of her lungs.

He hated the thought of her suffering, but Gill reminded him that all this was perfectly natural and that millions of women did this every second of every day.

Although that wasn't exactly true, as he quickly pointed out.

'Only about one hundred and thirty women gave birth to triplets in the UK according to the latest statistics. And having three babies is a much greater risk than having one. And, no doubt, more painful.'

'But Asher told us that Mia would be at the hospital within about ten minutes or so. And now she's in the ambulance, they'll be helping her with the pain and ensuring she's okay.'

That much was true, but Gill's reassuring words gave Jet little comfort.

Luckily, Jet and Gill arrived with minutes to spare, and Jet dashed to Mia's side.

Less than half an hour after her first contraction, Mia delivered a beautiful, baby girl with a smattering of midnight black hair.

Twenty minutes later a gorgeous baby boy arrived, screaming from the moment he breathed his first gulp of air. That terrified

Jet and clearly also Mia in spite of the fact she was about to give birth to yet another child. But the doctor assured them both, the baby boy was fine.

The third baby, also a boy, took a little longer but he too was fit and well.

Both boys, like their baby sister, had tiny circles of black hair, but one boy's hair was standing on end as if he had a Mohican, and Jet couldn't help but smile at that.

Jet's tears of joy took him by surprise. He had expected this experience to be emotional but he was unprepared for the sheer depth of feeling. His heart seemed to want to explode from his chest and he felt taller somehow and stronger. As if he had to be now that he had three babies to protect and cherish and keep safe from harm.

Being premature, the babies would be going to the neonatal unit for possibly several days, but both he and Mia were allowed to hold their children for a little while, as soon as the doctors and nurses had given the infants a good once over.

The proud parents were even allowed to take some photos, and Jet whipped out his phone and took several.

The two doctors who had been present pronounced that they didn't think the babies would need to be away from their parents for very long.

Unusually, for babies born in their thirty-fourth week, which was now how old they were, they weighed exactly five pounds each. The two boys each measured nearly eighteen inches and the girl was slightly shorter at seventeen and three-quarters.

All of them looked more like Jet than Mia. At least that's what their aunty Ella said when Jet sent her the photos via a message on his phone. And she also said, after congratulating them both, that she wasn't at all surprised by the weights of the babies, because, as she reminded Mia when Jet and Mia phoned her a little later.

'You were the size of a house and you did stuff yourself with chocolate cake in Seahorse Harbour.'

Names for the little girl were quickly chosen. Matilda Sarah Lori Cross, named after great aunt Mattie, Jet's deceased mum, Sarah, and Mia's own mum, Lori.

Names for the boys were proving more difficult. One of them would have the name Ernest, for Mia's long departed dad, but she didn't want Ernest as a first name. Jet hated his own dad, who had abandoned him and his beloved mum, so there was no way that man would get a mention.

They considered naming the boys after their male friends in Little Pondale but someone might feel left out, or wonder why their name wasn't first or whatever. Not that any of their friends probably would think that but Mia and Jet didn't want to take that chance.

Temporarily, the boys were merely called Jet Cross Two and Jet Cross Three. Mia and Jet didn't need to decide on names right away; they had forty-two days in which to do that and to register their babies, but they spent at least an hour tossing various names around, until Mia announced she needed sleep, and Jet and Gill dashed out to the nearest pub to celebrate.

Nineteen

'Have you heard the news?' Lilith Shoe dashed into The Seahorse Inn. 'Now I'm not one to gossip, as you know but—'

'We know,' Portia said, beaming at her. 'That is if you're about to say that one of my wedding planning team has had her babies.'

Lilith's shoulders slumped and the smile slid from her face. She seemed genuinely disappointed.

Portia waved her phone in the air. 'Bree's just called again. Mia had two boys and one girl, and mother and babies are in good health and doing well, in spite of the babies coming early.'

Portia could hardly believe it when Bree had called earlier to say they couldn't meet up for lunch because Mia was having her babies. Portia had been worried and so had Mikkel. The babies weren't due for a few more weeks, although Bree had told them triplets were usually early. But as Asher had told them when he'd come in for a well-earned drink, after ensuring Mia was safe and well in the ambulance, you can't stop nature doing its thing.

Now Bree had called again to give them all the good news and Mikkel had announced that the drinks were on the house to celebrate the birth of the triplets, only moments before Lilith had arrived.

But how Lilith knew about Mia was a mystery. Although, no doubt, someone at the sea life centre had probably told her.

Now Mikkel was leaning on the bar and smiling at Portia in a peculiar fashion.

'What's on your mind?' Portia asked, grinning with excitement.

'I was just wondering how it feels to be a dad,' he said. 'And hoping I might not have too long to wait to find out.'

'Oh, were you?' Portia laughed, hardly able to contain herself. 'Well it just so happens, I might have news for you on that very issue.'

He blinked several times. 'News? What news?'

She leant forward and kissed him across the bar. 'I haven't confirmed it yet, and I could be wrong. But I'm pretty sure I'm right. I realised, when Bree called earlier to tell us they had all gone to the hospital, that I haven't had my period. That makes me almost three weeks late. That could be down to the stress and excitement of planning this wedding ... or it could be something else. Bree, Mia and Ella all told me they knew they were pregnant before they took the test to confirm it. So let's just say, it's possibly a good thing we're getting married in only a matter of weeks, but I do need to take a test, to be certain.'

Mikkel's excited yell made everyone in The Seahorse Inn stop their conversations and stare in his direction.

Not that Mikkel seemed to care as he leapt over the bar and lifted Portia high into the air before kissing her far more passionately than he probably should have in such a public place.

Not that she cared either. All she cared about was that Mikkel loved her with all his heart; that they would be husband and wife in a matter of weeks, and perhaps, if she was right about her period and what that meant and how she felt, they would soon be even more than that.

They would be a family.

Twenty

Bree was glad to be home.

She had enjoyed her stay in Seahorse Harbour and had loved the Easterhill Hotel and Spa. There was a lot to be said for the luxury of a five-star hotel, for spa treatments, for a swimming pool just a stroll away from her room, for having drinks and meals prepared for her, for having people at her beck and call, for sleeping in a bed as soft as a cloud, and waking in the morning to the trill of birds and nothing else.

But none of that could compare to sleeping in her own bed beside the man she adored, or to waking up to the shrill cries of two infants and one extremely active youngster, or to Garrick swearing softly as he spilt coffee down his shirt as he tried to bring a cup to her while young Flora raced around his legs, sometimes with the added bruising power of her bright red, sit-in, racing car. Flora was no Lewis Hamilton, that was for sure, but she did love that car.

Bree had realised how much she missed this but now that she was home, she knew she never wanted to stay away from her family again. At least not for longer than one night.

She could handle the majority of the wedding plans from her cottage in Little Pondale, and Portia had already agreed that anything Bree couldn't handle from a distance, would be dealt with by Bethany, or Angela, or by Portia herself.

Ella was almost as excited as Bree was to be home but she told Bree later in the morning that she was having serious, spa withdrawal symptoms, so much so that Gill had agreed that the moment he finished his book – which would be within a week or two – they would spend a weekend at a luxury hotel to celebrate.

Mia was still in the hospital with her three newborns when Bree and Ella returned home. Due to the fact the babies were born early, as most triplets are, they would remain in neonatal care until it was established that they were ready to go home. Mia and Jet had been advised that this could be anything from eleven days upwards, but Mia and her babies were definitely the exception to that rule.

The babies had been declared fit and healthy at birth and within a matter of days – five days to be precise, an exuberant Mia and a euphoric Jet, brought their beautiful babies home to Little Pond Farm on day six, to be welcomed by the entire population of Little Pondale, lining their drive and waving flags, balloons and banners.

Baby gifts and congratulatory cards poured in. So many in fact that Mia told Bree, Ella, Garrick and Gill that it was a good thing she and Jet had several rooms in their home. One could be used to house all the gifts and toys and such.

'But not for long,' Jet said, wrapping an arm around Mia's shoulder as, with his other hand, he rocked the connected, triple cradles Garrick had made for the babies, and carved with beautifully intricate images of toys and stars and balloons. 'If Jezebella was right, and she has been so far, we'll need those rooms for the other two babies she said we would have.'

'Not so fast,' Mia said, giving him a loving smile. 'If you think I'm giving birth to another baby anytime soon, you can think again. I'll need at least a year, or maybe two to get over having these three. I know it was a miraculously easy birth and no one at the hospital could believe these were my first, but even so.'

Jet raised his brows, his huge smile quickly appearing. 'We're going to have sex again before a year though, aren't we?'

Mia, and everyone else, roared with laughter.

'We'll be having sex again the minute I'm comfortably able to do so,' she said. 'But you'll have to use protection because I'm serious about this, Jet. Having babies hurts. And besides, I'd quite like to be slim and attractive again for a while.'

'Phew!' He brushed his hand across his forehead, still smiling. 'That's a relief. About us having sex again, I mean. Not about you being slim and attractive. You'll always be beautiful to me.' His smile widened even further. 'Even if you are the size of a house, as Ella would say.' He kissed her then to prove his point.

'Well it's true,' Ella said. 'She was. Oh God you two. Get a room!'

Twenty-One

Elsie dashed into Seahorse Bites Café, her long locks of purple hair tumbling from the bright red, beaded ribbon with which she'd tied them into a loose bun, and her sunshine yellow cotton, longline shirt flapping around her white jeans and matching T-shirt.

'Josie!' she shrieked. 'Where's Diana? Have you seen her? Have you heard the news? Oh dear Lord. I sound like Lilith Shoe.' She collapsed on to the chair opposite Josie who was sitting at their usual table in the window. 'But this is serious.'

'What's wrong? You look as if you're about to have a heart attack.'

Josie reached out her hand and placed her fingers on Elsie's wrist.

Elsie tutted and brushed Josie's hand away.

'I'm not having a heart attack. But Diana might.' She leant forward and looked around her, lowering her voice to just a whisper. 'Portia's pregnant.'

'Portia's pregnant!' Josie's voice boomed out.

Elsie shook her head and sighed.

'Good job on keeping that a secret, honeybee.'

Josie looked apologetic, but luckily only tourists appeared to be occupying the other tables, and Lyn, Sorcha and Nathan were all beavering away in the kitchen, out of range.

'Sorry,' Josie said, lowering her voice. 'That was such a surprise. I don't think there's anyone here who knows them though, so the secret should be safe. But are you sure? How do you even know that? Don't tell me. Lilith Shoe has been gossiping again.'

'No. Oddly enough she hasn't. At least not within my earshot. Do you remember Mikkel's dad, Gray? Of course you do. He was here last summer.'

'Yes. I remember him. You and he were ... *friends*.' Josie threw her a suggestive smile.

'We still are,' Elsie said, with a reproachful look. 'That's how I know about Portia. Mikkel told his dad last night and his dad told me this morning. About five minutes ago in fact.'

187

'He called you from Hell?'

Hell, in Norway was where Mikkel's father lived, and where Mikkel himself had grown up. The residents of Seahorse Harbour always made a joke of it but some people didn't realise that Hell was indeed a real place and thought they were referring to the fire and brimstone Hell instead.

'Yes. He often does. Don't give me that look, honeybee. He called to let me know he'll be coming over for the wedding. He's leaving Hell in a couple of weeks, and he plans to stay for a month or two. Portia and Mikkel will be off on their honeymoon and he's going to be looking after Mikkel's house.' She waved her arms in the air. 'That's not important. What is important is Portia being pregnant. How will Diana take that news when she finds out? And she will find out. Nothing remains a secret for long in Seahorse Harbour.'

'Or in Hell, it seems.' Josie smirked. 'Was he supposed to tell you? I'm surprised Mikkel hasn't mentioned it to Liam.'

'Of course he wasn't supposed to tell me,' Elsie whispered, as a stranger moved within earshot of their table.

The woman, who definitely wasn't local, appeared to be looking at the display of leaflets, one of which was for Fulbright Ceramics. Josie smiled at her as she glanced in their direction and the woman smiled back, but there must have been something about her because Josie looked at Elsie and placed a finger to her lips.

Elsie got the message and stared out across the bay while Josie pretended to be looking at something on her phone until the woman returned to her table, several feet away.

'Sorry,' Josie said. 'I didn't want to take any chances. What were you saying?'

Elsie peered over her shoulder. The woman was still looking in their direction but she completely ignored Elsie's stare as if she were looking past their table and out towards the bay.

'I was saying it's meant to be a secret until after the wedding. Not because they're ashamed or embarrassed or anything, but simply because they don't want that fact overshadowing their Big Day. But I knew from Gray's tone that there was something he was dying to say. He sounded far more excited than usual. I was sure it wasn't just about the upcoming nuptials, so I pressed the point and eventually he let the cat out of the bag. Naturally, I assured him I wouldn't tell a soul.'

Josie laughed. 'And yet you are.'

Elsie frowned. 'Of course I am. But only you. And only because I'm worried about

Diana. She's been coping rather well since that incident at the hotel last week.' Josie had told Elsie about Diana trying to kiss Mikkel on the lips in the Easterhill Hotel bar. 'And then that wedding planner, Mia, having her babies meant everyone was talking about that and not about the wedding, so Diana seemed to relax. But now this has happened and I'm concerned that when Diana hears the news, she might ...'

'Have some sort of relapse?'

'Yes. Exactly that. What should we do?'

Josie seemed to consider the matter for a moment.

'We'll have to tell her. As you said, someone is bound to find out. It's far better if she hears this news from us.'

Elsie nodded. 'I agree. But when?'

'What about this afternoon? I was going to her place later anyway, so it won't seem as if I've gone there for some special reason. We'll see what sort of mood she's in and we'll take it from there.'

'We? Am I going too?'

'Yes. If I tell her, it's gossip. If you tell her, you're simply repeating the news from Mikkel's dad. We'll say we bumped into one another and you decided to tag along.'

Elsie pulled a face. 'Oh wonderful. I do so enjoy being the bearer of bad news.'

'I'm sorry, Elsie. I know how you feel, but I think that's for the best.'

'Fine. But can we stop off at The Seahorse Inn on the way? I'll need something stronger than coffee if I've got to tell Diana.' She glanced around as Josie nodded. 'Talking of coffee, where is everyone? I could die of thirst here.'

Josie sighed. 'They're all in the kitchen. Sorcha and Asher have spoken to their parents and made it clear that a double wedding for Sorcha and Nathan and Lottie and Asher isn't going to happen. Now Sorcha, Nathan and Lyn are checking their calendars and discussing various dates.'

'Finally,' Elsie said. 'I wonder if Lottie knows that yet. Asher must have told her. I expect she'll let me know today. We'll also need to discuss some dates. But why the long face, honeybee?'

Josie slumped forward and plonked her forearms on the table.

'Because no matter how many hints I drop about everyone in this bloody village getting married, Liam just won't seem to take the bait.'

Twenty-Two

So, Portia Trulove was pregnant, was she?

The woman stared at the purple-haired pensioner-cum-teenage-wanna-be and the pretty young woman with chestnut-coloured hair sitting at the table in the window, and sneered.

She was certain that was what the young woman had said. She hadn't misheard that little snippet, she was sure of that. Her ears had been tuned for any piece of news about that bitch, Portia. But then the women had lowered their voices and she hadn't been able to hear much more.

She had heard mention of Mikkel's dad and of Hell, but had no idea what those two things had in common and even when she got up and pretended to be looking at those crappy leaflets, she still couldn't hear a word they said.

And it seemed that the young woman may have been suspicious because they had both fallen silent until she had returned to her seat.

Now she couldn't hear a thing.

But that didn't really matter. She'd heard something far juicier than she could've hoped for and now she had her headline for tomorrow's column.

'Wedding Bells for Portia Trulove – but only because she's Up the Duff.'

She emptied her coffee cup, tossed a few coins on the table, pushed her chair back, and sauntered out of the café, smiling at the two unwitting sources, as she went.

Twenty-Three

Diana took the news of Portia's pregnancy far better than Josie or Elsie had obviously expected.

At least that was the impression she gave. But once they had left, it was a different matter.

She screamed, she cried, she threw things.

Henry watched her intently from his vantage point on the sofa. He even joined in and barked so loud he drowned out Diana's swearing.

That made her stop for a moment and stare at him. Was she frightening him? She hadn't meant to do that.

She took several deep breaths and tried to calm down. But that didn't seem to be working. Instead she marched to the wine cooler, took out a perfectly chilled bottle of her favourite Sancerre and, once the cork was removed, gulped down at least half the contents directly from the bottle.

'Classy,' she said, thumping the bottle on to the kitchen counter and wiping a trickle of wine from her chin. She sucked in a deep breath and pulled herself up straight. 'The only way from here is down, unless I do something about this, Henry.'

Quite what she could do, she had no idea, but drinking wine directly from a bottle was too much for her sensibilities.

As was causing a scene in the village pub.

And smashing Mikkel's windscreen.

And trying to kiss someone else's fiancé in a hotel bar.

She turned towards the sofa, hesitated for a second, and turned back and grabbed the bottle.

'I've started, so I'll finish. I'm going to drown my sorrows today, Henry, and wallow in self-pity. But tomorrow I'm going to get up, get dressed, and get back to the woman I once was. I don't think I like the woman I've become.'

Twenty-Four

Bethany was speaking to Angela via her iPad as Portia sauntered into Mikkel's kitchen. Even though Portia lived with him now she still sometimes thought of their home as his.

She was about to say, 'Good morning' but there was something in Bethany's tone that made Portia feel it might not be a *good* morning after all.

'I think she needs to know,' Bethany said.

'Does she?' queried Angela, sounding equally concerned. 'She only told me two days ago that she was pregnant. How the heck did BB find out?'

'BB? Is that her name?'

'No. That's just what I call her and so does Portia now. It stands for Big Bitch. But what good would come of telling Portia about this? She might ignore the horrid things the bloody woman says about her but I'm sure, deep down, it must have some effect. We don't want to ruin her wedding plans, do we?'

Portia coughed and smiled wanly as Bethany's head shot round, a look of horror on her face, which matched Angela's expression on the iPad screen.

'I ... I didn't hear you come in,' Bethany stammered.

'Hi Portia. How are you on this sunny morning?' Angela was trying to sound bright and breezy but the anxiety on her face and in her tone belied her words.

Portia walked to the fridge, the weak smile still on her lips.

'Morning you two. I'm fine thanks.' She opened the fridge door and took out a bottle of freshly squeezed orange juice, which she knew had been delivered to the door that day. Mikkel ordered juice and milk and butter and cheese from the nearby dairy farm. It was a relatively new venture by the farmer, apparently after having supplied the village during a severe snow storm at Christmas, and all the residents were supporting it. 'At least I was.'

'You heard, didn't you?' Bethany said.

'Oh God,' said Angela.

'I did,' Portia confirmed. 'But I'm not sure what it was about so perhaps you'd fill me in. I heard something about me being pregnant, and I suspect I can safely assume that a certain tabloid columnist has somehow uncovered that news and written some unpleasant things about me, yet again.'

'She has,' Angela said. 'But it's just the same old rubbish and I don't think you should read it. It astonishes me that the bloody paper prints her stuff.'

'I'd rather know what's been said and then I can ignore it.'

Bethany and Angela exchanged glances via the screen.

'Okay.'

Bethany pressed a few keys and Angela's face popped up in one corner while a page of vitriol filled the remainder of the screen.

'The headline's naff,' Portia said, forcing a smile while she read. 'And the rest of it doesn't seem to improve.' She looked away long before the end. 'You're right. It's better if I don't read that. I didn't get pregnant "to entrap Mikkel" and certainly not so that I could get my hands on Seahorse Harbour Holiday Park.'

'Of course you didn't!' Angela snapped. 'We all know that. The woman is just an evil bitch.'

Portia laughed mirthlessly. 'But she is right about Mikkel being far too good for me.'

'Er. That isn't the only thing she says.' Bethany scrolled and stopped a few paragraphs down. 'She twists that sentence further on and says he "seems to be far too good to be true", and then she goes on to tear him off a strip or two over his affair with a married woman. Sorry, Portia.'

'Oh God. No. She doesn't talk about Diana, does she?' Portia speed-read the paragraphs and dropped on to the chair beside her sister. 'How did she find out all this stuff?' She met Bethany's eyes before darting a look at Angela's face on the screen. 'You ... you don't think she's here, do you? In Seahorse Harbour.'

'She can't be,' Bethany said.

Angela hesitated. 'She could be. I think she'll go to any lengths to hurt you. Is there somewhere local that she could stay without you knowing?'

Portia shook her head. 'Not really. The only places to stay in the village are the Holiday Park, Mikkel's boathouse, and ... Oh God. That would explain how she found out about most of this. But not about me being pregnant. Because Lilith doesn't know that. She couldn't, could she?'

Bethany shrugged as Portia stared at her. 'From what you've said about Lilith Shoe, anything is possible.'

'Who is Lilith Shoe?' Angela asked.

'The local gossip,' Bethany said.

Portia sighed. 'And she owns the Sunrise B&B.'

'Then that could very well be where BB is staying.'

'If she is,' Portia said, 'she won't be there for long. Lilith may be a dreadful gossip but she doesn't mean to hurt anyone. Even though she often does. If she reads this and realises that this hurts not just me but also Mikkel, Diana and more importantly to her, Diana's family, I'm fairly certain she'll toss the woman out the door.'

Bethany smiled. 'Then I'll make sure Lilith sees it.' She jumped off her chair and raced towards the door, turning back to grab her iPad. 'I'll need this, so we'll have to say goodbye for now, Angela.'

'Oh. Okay. Bye. Portia! I'll call you right now.'

She only just managed to finish the sentence before Bethany closed the iPad cover.

Twenty-Five

It wasn't long before Bethany returned, with a huge smile on her face.

'You were right about BB staying at the Sunrise B&B, Portia. You were also right about Lilith Shoe. She was livid when I showed her the column. Oh. But there was one tiny issue. She didn't know you're pregnant.'

'She didn't?'

'No. But now she does. Sorry.'

Portia let out a loud sigh. 'It's okay. She would've found out sooner or later.'

'She was actually quite cross that she didn't know. She went on and on about it for at least five minutes. Until I explained that you being pregnant wasn't the issue at hand. It was the damage this column would do that was the problem. She may be small – and rather odd-looking. Almost like a clown in some ways. But she's got a temper on her, hasn't she?'

'Has she? I don't think I've ever seen her angry.'

Bethany laughed. 'Take it from me, you don't want to.'

'What did she say?'

Bethany laughed louder. 'What *didn't* she say? The air turned blue. She stormed upstairs. I waited downstairs out of sight. I didn't want tomorrow's column to be about your sister calling in the heavies or something. Anyway, Lilith banged on the door to BB's room and screamed at her. "This is a highly respectable B&B and I'm not having the likes of you sullying my sheets and besmirching my good name with your trashy diatribe. If you're not out of this establishment within thirty minutes, I'll get some friends of mine to throw you out. And I'm still charging your credit card for your stay so don't think I'm not. Now get out of here before I slap your face this side of ninepence." I have no clue what that means but it had the desired effect. BB swore at Lilith and Lilith swore back. BB threatened to sue and Lilith said she had friends in much higher places than the gutter, which was obviously where the woman lived, so to go ahead, because she relished a good fight. And she'd never lost one yet. I assume that was all bluster, but who knows.'

Portia laughed in spite of the situation.

'Oh I almost wish I'd been there.'

'I think the rest of Lilith's guests enjoyed it. They all clapped when Lilith went into the breakfast room and explained. Don't worry. She didn't tell them all the details. She said, "I'm not one to gossip, so I can't fill you in on what that was about, but I will say that the woman wrote some exceedingly unpleasant things about some people I care very much about and I'm not having that kind of person staying under my roof." I suspect they'll all be on their best behaviour for the durations of their stays.

'I wish you'd recorded it, so I could hear Lilith,' Portia said between her laughter.

'I did. Which is how I know precisely what Lilith said. I listened to it twice on my way back here. I'll play it for you and Angela now. Let's call her back.'

'Brilliant! Oh. But what happened then? I assume BB has left the building.'

'With her tail tightly between her legs. Lilith held the door open for her and told her not to darken the door again. Or to stay anywhere else in Seahorse Harbour. "Lowlifes like you aren't welcome in this village", she said and slammed the door behind BB as she was still walking out. I'm pretty sure she almost fell down the steps. I have to say, I like Lilith a lot. I know you said she's a gossip, but wow. She sticks up for people she cares about. BB could sue her. But Lilith genuinely didn't seem to care.'

'I think I like her too. But remind me not to read BB's column tomorrow.'

'Ooh. That's another thing Lilith said. She said a good friend of hers knows the owner of the tabloid paper BB writes for. Lilith's going to make a few calls.'

Portia frowned at that. 'I'm not sure Lilith or her friend have any influence with the owner of the paper. As far as I'm aware, her friend, Doreen is a cleaner at the local newspaper in Easterhill. But if they do, I hope they won't try to get BB fired. I don't like her or what she writes about me but I don't want her to lose her job. She's already lost enough.'

BB hated Portia with a vengeance and although Portia wasn't entirely sure why, the only reason she'd ever been able to come up with was that BB's now ex-husband had asked Portia out several times. Portia had always said no because she didn't date married men, but BB seemed to blame Portia for the breakdown of her marriage and vitriolic comments soon began to appear.

Angela had often suggested that Portia should take BB to court, but Portia believed it was better to ignore it.

BB was clearly bitter and extremely unhappy. She'd lost the man she loved and she seemed to blame Portia for some reason. Portia could live with that because she knew she'd done nothing wrong. Yes, people would read the rubbish BB wrote, but it was just one newspaper and one small column. People would believe what they wanted to believe. Suing BB would only fan the flames by adding fuel to the fire. Portia had always believed most people had better things to do than read the rantings of one woman.

'You're too nice for your own good,' Bethany said.

Portia didn't agree with that, but she was relieved and thankful when she later discovered Doreen did have influence with the owner of that particular newspaper. Quite a lot of influence it seemed.

The paper printed a retraction of the column the following day and an apology for any unintended offence it may have caused. That was a pretty big thing. It also stated that the columnist was "taking a short break but will be back next month with a new column on the joys and health benefits of gardening".

Portia enjoyed a spot of gardening, but she wasn't certain that BB did.

At least now, perhaps, BB's future columns wouldn't mention Portia.

Unless BB named a slug or some other garden pest after her. Which wouldn't surprise Portia at all.

Twenty-Six

It didn't take long for news to spread around the village; both about Lilith's eviction of her undesirable guest, and of the fact that Portia was pregnant. Everyone knew about both by the following day. The day the retraction was printed.

Josie was very glad that she and Elsie had known about the pregnancy beforehand and that they'd decided to tell Diana, but when Orla showed her a photo of the woman who had written the column that Lilith had been so incensed about, Josie wasn't quite so pleased.

'I feel so guilty,' she told Elsie later that afternoon as they sat in Elsie's beautiful garden sipping her famous elderflower cordial, which was equal measures of cordial and gin and the perfect drink for a hot, summer day.

Bees buzzed busily around, collecting nectar from a carpet of flowers that swayed gently back and forth as if they were dancing their own form of a floral rumba, and the heavenly scent of lavender wafted through the air.

Josie, Elsie and Lottie sat in Lloyd loom garden chairs around the table beneath the grapevine as a couple of blackbirds sang from the trees and a bluetit and a sparrow splashed about in the stone birdbath on the lawn.

'Why?' Elsie asked, tipping her large vivid orange sunhat back slightly so that she could see Josie's face.

'Because that was the woman who was in Seahorse Bites Café. The one who came over and stood near our table. Do you think she overheard our conversation? Did she get that news from us? Well from me, I suppose because I was the one who shouted it so loud that someone on the coast of France could hear.'

'Possibly,' Elsie said. 'But she is a columnist and they have sources, don't they? She might have got that information from somewhere else.'

'Except you and I were the only ones who knew, outside of Portia and Mikkel's families.'

'You don't know that for a fact,' Lottie said. 'Portia has friends. She may have told one of them.'

'Perhaps. But I think it's a bit of a coincidence, don't you?' Josie looked at Elsie. 'Should I apologise to Portia?'

'What? No, honeybee. As far as we're aware she has no idea that the woman was in the café and therefore no suspicions about us. I think we should keep quiet about the whole thing and play dumb if anyone asks. It's not as if anyone we knew saw the woman near our table. No. I think it's best to leave that can of worms unopened. And not just for our benefit but for Gray's too. We don't want to get him in trouble with Mikkel and Portia for telling me about it. More importantly, has Diana seen the column? And Alex?'

'Yep. And also Becca. Someone at her boarding school saw it online and showed her. Toby hasn't seen it yet, as far as Di knows but she was in a right state when she called me to ask if I'd seen it too. She was crying and shouting and sobbing. She said she wanted to curl up and die. But as I told her, everyone knew about the affair between her and Mikkel, so that was hardly news. And besides, the paper has printed a retraction, which kind of says that most of what was in that column probably isn't true. That's what I told Di, anyway, and that seemed to make her slightly happier. Admittedly, it might be embarrassing for Alex if his work colleagues or patients or such read the column, and I accept that it wasn't very nice for darling Becca, but again, Becca knew about Di and Mikkel and she's not a teenager who is fazed by gossip. Di said Alex doesn't look at tabloids and neither does anyone they know, but she called him and told him about it and he's rearranged his day so that he can come down and be with Di.'

'That's a good thing,' Lottie said.

'It's the best thing for Di, that's for sure. I offered to go and be with her but she got a text from Alex while we were talking and he said he'd be there soon.'

'So this whole thing might simply blow over?' Elsie asked.

'Let's hope so. Once the gossip in the village has died down.'

Which didn't take long at all, because the day after that, Sorcha and Nathan announced they had set their date, and so did Lottie and Asher, followed only hours later by Lucy and Kev announcing theirs. The weddings were to be in September, October and November, respectively, with Portia's at the end of June.

After that, all everyone was talking about was which bride would have the best dress, the best cake, the best bouquet, the best wedding reception and so on.

Naturally, due to Portia's wealth, most people assumed it would be her, but then someone mentioned Portia's somewhat unusual cake and tongues started wagging about what a wedding cake should look like – and it wasn't at all like Portia's.

'It's odd that no one's getting married in July or August,' Josie said when she heard.

This time she, Elsie and Lottie were having lunch in The Seahorse Inn.

'You could,' Elsie joked.

Josie rolled her eyes and sighed.

'I wish.'

Lottie said, 'Asher wanted ours to be after the end of the tourist season. Summer is busy for him and the rest of The Seahorse Riders.'

'Yeah.' Josie nodded. 'That's what Liam said. But Mikkel's one and he's getting married this month. Kev isn't a Seahorse Rider and Lucy's a school teacher. I would've thought the summer would be a perfect time for them, what with the school holidays.'

'True. I can't wait to get married.' Lottie beamed at Josie. 'Sorry to rub that in.'

'Don't apologise. It's not your fault that Liam doesn't appear to want me for his wife.'

'That's nonsense, honeybee.' Elsie slapped Josie on the hand. 'Give him time. He'll get around to it.'

'Yeah. But when? I'd quite like to still have all my own teeth when I'm a bride.'

Twenty-Seven

Due to the fact that Portia was pregnant, the bridal shower that Bethany arranged and the hen party organised by Angela were rather more sober affairs than originally planned. The bridal shower was held in Mikkel's restaurant and the hen party in his nightclub.

But both events nearly didn't happen. Someone called the local authority and made a complaint about the food hygiene standards in Hippocampus and an inspector turned up to check the restaurant for cleanliness and food safety just the day before the bridal shower. Luckily, it was someone Mikkel knew and it was clear the call was unwarranted, so although the man still carried out his inspection, the restaurant remained open.

When the fire brigade was called to Neptune's nightclub on the very evening of the hen party due to potential fire hazards, Josie said that, unless she was mistaken, either Fate – or someone, had it in for Portia and Mikkel.

Both events eventually went off without any further hitches but neither were quite as much fun as Josie had expected. Diana wasn't invited to either, but Lottie was, and she agreed with Josie.

'Perhaps rich people don't get as drunk as we ordinary mortals do,' Josie said. 'But having said that, Di's rich and she does.'

'You don't need to be drunk to have fun,' Elsie said.

Josie gave her an odd look. 'Says the woman who puts alcohol in everything.'

'I think the restaurant complaint and then the fire call-out put a bit of a dampener on them,' Lottie said. 'I haven't arranged my hen party yet and I suppose I ought to, but I hope nothing like that happens on mine.'

'Do you think both things were just a coincidence? Elsie asked.

Josie shrugged. 'Who knows? But I think it's pretty unlikely, don't you? I did wonder about Diana. I know that sounds awful but I wasn't the only one who thought that. I heard Portia's sister mention Di, but Portia's friend Angela said they mustn't jump to conclusions and that there was someone else who might stoop to something like that. I have a feeling they were referring to that columnist.'

'I wonder if something will go wrong on the actual wedding day?' Lottie said.

Josie was wondering the same thing.

Twenty-Eight

As luck would have it, nothing else went wrong prior to the wedding day. Partly because everything was checked and double checked and checked again, and partly because Bethany and Angela, and more importantly, Bree made sure that any possible issues could be handled quickly and quietly, no matter what they might be.

Tommy Trulove even had his own security team drafted in, just in case, but thankfully they weren't needed.

Mia and Jet Cross declined their invitations to the wedding, having their hands full with three very loud, but wonderful babies. Ella, Gill, Bree and Garrick attended, Bree and Ella arriving on the Thursday before the Big Day, and Garrick and Gill joined them on Friday evening for the wedding on Saturday. Mia and Jet, with a great deal of help from Mia's mum, Lori and her new stepdad, Franklin, along with Hettie and Fred had also offered to look after Flora and the twins so that Bree and Garrick would be child-free for the weekend.

'What difference can three more kids make?' Mia said.

Bree hoped she wouldn't regret those words, but accepted the very kind offer even though doing so gave her cause for concern. Not because she didn't trust Mia and Jet and the others to take exceptionally good care of her children, but because she didn't particularly want to be parted from them again.

'It's only for two nights, darling,' Garrick said. 'And I'll be with them for one of those.'

'It's not that I'm worried about,' Bree said. 'It's the fact I don't want to be away from them. I missed them so much last time. But you're right. I know you are. And it is only for two nights. That will fly and I'll be home with them again soon enough.'

On the wedding day itself, the sun shone from first thing in the morning until the final rays sunk beneath the horizon that night, which was a great relief to everyone as it had rained for almost the entire week beforehand.

'Rain's a bad omen,' Lilith had said.

Some felt that Diana would have been disappointed that the weather turned out fine.

The flowers in St Mary Star of the Sea were nothing short of magnificent. Simple white daisies and yellow roses vied for attention with tropical blooms and exotic plants that were a rainbow of colours. The perfumes of many of them competed with the multitude of perfumes worn by the wedding guests.

Portia and Tommy walked down the aisle to Savage Garden's, *I Knew I Loved You*, sung by a professional singer from Bree's list and accompanied by a string quartet. Savage Garden were one of Mikkel's favourite bands.

Portia looked beautiful. Her wedding dress was elegant and understated; ivory silk, off the shoulder with a fitted waist and a heart-shaped train. Although the dress had needed a slight alteration on the day before the wedding due to Portia having put on a tiny bit of weight. Bree ensured that was dealt without the slightest fuss. Portia also wore a veil and a floral headdress and Bethany and Angela wore pale blue silk gowns of equal elegance and simplicity.

Mikkel wore a morning suit as did his best man, Jonno, and a blue tie that matched the bridesmaids' dresses, plus a smile as wide as the ocean.

When Perse, the Reverend, asked if anyone had any reason why the couple should not be married, all eyes turned to the door.

But Diana didn't burst in, as some people half expected. Josie had already told Bree that Diana and Alex had left the week before on an exotic holiday Alex had booked, just for the two of them. They were also stopping off on the way, to visit Becca and Noah whose exciting news had been that they were spending the summer working at an olive farm in Italy. Toby had gone to a camp with his Air Cadets and Henry had stayed with Josie and Liam. Bree hadn't needed to know all that but Josie had told her anyway.

Twenty-Nine

After the wedding ceremony, Liam suggested that he and Josie should take Henry for a quick walk. There was to be an informal lunch at The Seahorse Inn, but that was mainly for those who hadn't been invited to either the wedding breakfast, or to the main wedding reception in the evening in the marquees in Mikkel's garden. Josie and Liam were invited to both, as were Orla and her boyfriend, Darren, so skipping the lunch meant Liam and Josie could have some time to themselves. At least that's what Liam told Josie.

They went to Little Wood and walked hand in hand between the trees as Henry chased shadows or the occasional squirrel.

'So,' Liam said, 'Portia and Mikkel are married. Lottie and Asher have set their date for October as they'd planned, in spite of that meaning that Sorcha and Nathan's wedding will be before theirs. That's booked for the last weekend in September. And Lucy and Kev's is in November.'

Josie threw him a questioning look. 'I know. We've known that for a couple of weeks now.'

'I know we have. I'm simply saying it's a busy year, as far as weddings go.'

'Oh. Well you're forgetting Molly Ford and Chance Warren,' Josie said, with a small sigh. 'And Molly's brother Terry and his fiancée, Sarah. They're also getting married. In September and October, respectively.'

'Ah. But they're marrying in Easterhill, not here.'

'And your point is?'

He stopped beneath a copper beech tree. Their copper beech tree. The one beneath which they'd made love for the very first time, in a thunderstorm, last year.

Sometimes it seemed to Josie that more than just one year had gone by since that day. Other times it felt like only yesterday that Liam had told her how much he loved her.

He patted the trunk with one hand, smiled at Josie and got down on one knee.

Producing a small velvet-covered box from his pocket, he said, 'My point is, isn't it about time we did the same? Will you marry me, Josie Parnell? Will you make me the

221

happiest man in Seahorse Harbour and agree to be my wife?' He lifted the lid and a massive diamond ring sparkled in the dappled rays as the leaves of the copper beech gently rustled as if they were quietly cheering.

Josie couldn't speak. She'd waited for this day for so long but now that it was here she couldn't quite believe it.

Liam's brows furrowed and a nervous smile hovered on his lips.

'You do want to marry me, don't you? I haven't got this completely wrong, have I?'

'No!' She shrieked. 'I mean, yes! No, you haven't got it wrong and yes, I definitely want to marry you. One hundred and ten per cent yes.'

'Thank God for that,' Liam said, getting to his feet and pulling her into his arms. 'Mikkel's booked us the bridal suite at the Easterhill Hotel and Spa for tonight and tomorrow so that we can celebrate in style. After their wedding reception is over, of course. I had to ask him to do it because I know you're friends with two of the receptionists there and I didn't want them to ruin the surprise. And before you ask, Orla and Darren have agreed to look after Henry. I'm sure you don't mind the fact that I had to ask Orla if she was completely happy about this before I proposed to you. Not about looking after Henry. About me asking you to marry me.'

'Of course I don't mind.' Josie laughed ecstatically as she slid her arms around Liam's neck. 'But what exactly did she say? I'm just curious.'

He furrowed his brows. 'She said, "Oh my god, Dad. Finally. What has taken you so long?" Or something very similar to that.'

'She took the words right out of my mouth,' Josie said. 'What has taken you so long?' But she was beaming at him as she said it.

Liam shook his head. 'I'm not entirely sure. Partly, because the Josie I fell in love with wasn't that interested in marriage, or so she said at first.' He grinned at her but soon became serious. 'And partly because of what Una did. And then because she had died. It took me some time to get over her betrayal and then the guilt over her death.'

'You had nothing to feel guilty for.'

He shrugged. 'I know. But I still did. I didn't think I'd ever get married again.' He pulled her closer. 'And then you came into my life. Our lives. It didn't take long for me to realise that I wanted to spend the rest of my life with you. I just wasn't sure you felt the same.'

'I told you I did!'

'I know. But I couldn't quite believe it. And then, once we were living together it didn't seem to matter quite so much if we were married or not. But it did to you, didn't it? Yes. I got the hints. Eventually. I wish you'd said something outright. But even before your hints, I was planning to propose to you at Christmas. Except all that stuff happened with Diana and Alex so it didn't seem the right time.'

'At Christmas? You were going to propose to me?'

'I was. I changed it to Valentine's Day, but then Lottie and Asher were getting engaged, so I delayed it yet again. Easter seemed good, but then there was yet another drama with Diana, so I postponed it once more. This time I was determined that no matter what, I was going to do it this month. And then Portia and Mikkel announced their wedding. But that wasn't going to stop me again. So I went ahead and asked Mikkel to book the room.'

Josie's mouth fell open and she slapped him on the arm.

'All this time ... All these months, I've been wondering why you wouldn't propose and the entire time you'd been planning to? Why didn't you simply do it?'

'I told you why. Plus I wanted it to be perfect. Okay. I accept that maybe this isn't perfect. Proposing to you by a tree while we're walking your sister's dog on someone else's wedding day, but I was determined it would be today.'

'This is pretty perfect to me. But you could've proposed to me beside a dustbin and I'd have been as happy. All I want is to be your wife. Well, maybe that's not all I want.'

'Oh? There's something else?' He eyed her with a huge grin on his face. 'Am I going to like this?'

'I don't know. I hope so. It's something I've been thinking about for a while.' She looked him in the eye. 'I know we have Orla and I love her to bits, but ... how do you feel about having another child?'

'How do I feel about that?' He beamed at her. 'Let me show you how I feel.'

He kissed her then, so passionately that she forgot they were standing beside a copper beech tree in Little Wood, just before midday on a Saturday. But most people in the village were attending one or other of Portia and Mikkel's wedding celebrations at some stage today so they'd probably all have better things to do than be wandering around in the wood.

She tugged at Liam's jacket and tossed it to the ground. He slid his hand beneath her dress and she wriggled free of her knickers.

225

He lifted her up so that her legs were wrapped around him, just as they had been that first time they had made love on this very spot. But today, dappled sunshine pierced the trees, not torrential rain.

'Oh wait!' She teased her lips from his and grinned. 'At the risk of ruining this moment, can we please pick up my knickers? Henry is running around here somewhere and you know what happened last time.'

Liam laughed at that, but he gently placed her feet back on the ground, bent down and retrieved her knickers and slid them into his trouser pocket.

'Now where was I?' he said, lifting her up once more.

'You were telling me how you felt about us having another child,' Josie said.

'Ah yes. And in case you're in any doubt. My response to that is, yes. I'd love to have a child with you.'

'Now that,' she said, 'is definitely the perfect proposal.'

Thirty

The bell tinkled above the door of Seahorse Bites Café as Tommy Trulove entered.

'Be with you in just a jiffy,' Lyn called out from the kitchen 'Sit anywhere you like.'

Tommy smiled and sat at the table by the window; the one he'd sat at a few weeks earlier and waited for Lyn to appear. It was a wet Monday morning and the café was half empty but the aromas from the kitchen were enough to cheer up the customers who had ventured out.

What a good thing the weather held off until after his daughter's wedding.

'Oh. It's you.' Lyn appeared from the kitchen and smiled at him. 'Hello. I thought you'd be long gone by now. Did the bride and groom get off on their exotic honeymoon?'

'They did.'

'It was a beautiful wedding, Tommy.'

'It was. And it got me thinking.'

She eyed him curiously.

'I hope you're not considering wedding number ... what would it be?'

'Seven, I believe. I'm told I've had five more wives since the one who really mattered to me passed away. But no. No more weddings for me. Not unless I ever find a woman who I can happily grow old with.'

Lyn laughed. 'I hate to ruin your day, but you're old now.'

He shrugged. 'You're only as old as you feel, so they say.'

She slid on to the chair opposite and sighed.

'I feel very old today. I think I need a holiday.'

He grinned at her. 'That's another thing I was thinking.' He reached into his jacket pocket and pulled out two tickets which he placed on the table. 'No strings. No complications. No promises. Just a long, luxury holiday with an old friend, which would, at some stage, include a round the world cruise. But we have to be careful to avoid specific areas at certain times. Being on a ship during hurricane season is not something either of us would enjoy. I thought, perhaps, we could cruise and stay, and cruise and stay some more. I can show you every one of our Trulove hotels, along the way. What do you say? Are you ready for an adventure, Lyn?'

She stared at the tickets and her mouth fell open. Slowly, she raised her eyes to meet his.

'A luxury holiday and a world cruise? With you, you mean?'

'Unless you'd prefer to go with someone else, in which case, that's fine. Consider it a gift.'

'No.' She smiled. 'There's no one else I'd rather go with. But are you sure? I'll pay my way, you know.'

He laughed. 'I'm sure. And no, you won't. This is my treat and it's all on me. No arguing about that.'

She narrowed her eyes. 'And no funny business?'

He shook his head and crossed his heart.

'No funny business, I promise. Separate suites. Both in the hotels and on the ships.'

'Suites? We'll have suites?'

'Absolutely. We're doing this in style. Next door to one another though.' He grinned. 'Now that I'm old, I try not to walk too far unless it's a necessity.'

She grinned at him and got to her feet.

'When would we have to leave?'

He shrugged. 'Whenever it's convenient. These plane tickets are to Rome and they depart next week. But I can change the dates.

I thought Rome was a good place to start, especially as we have a particularly lovely hotel there. From Rome, we can go wherever we like. Several ships cruise the world from various ports, so I'm sure we'll find something to suit. Or at least, my secretary will.'

'Next week is fine with me. I would have to check with Nathan though. And I'd need to be back in time for his wedding. That's the last weekend in September.'

Tommy nodded. 'Or we could fly back for that and continue our holiday once the happy couple have departed on their honeymoon. Unless you need to be here to run the café?'

Lyn laughed and rubbed her chin. 'Let me think. Run the café or travel the world? Hmmm. That's a difficult choice. I think I can risk closing the café until Sorcha and Nathan get back. And the tourist season will be over by then, so it's really not a major issue. But ... what if you get sick of me? Or I get sick of you? Or we don't get on?'

Now Tommy laughed and shook his head. 'Do you think that's likely?'

'You have had six wives, Tommy.' She winked at him.

'Good point. Then we'd definitely better not get married or do anything foolish like that. And I'll make sure you have an open ticket to fly home from anywhere in the world, so if you do want to up and leave me, you'll have the means to do so.'

Lyn beamed at him. 'Well, okay then. And thank you. Thank you from the bottom of my heart. This means a lot, you know.'

'It's my pleasure, Lyn. I think this holiday will do us both some good.'

'I'm looking forward to it already. Now what can I get you? Poached egg on toast and a pot of tea? And this is my treat, so no arguing about that.'

Tommy laughed louder. 'That sounds perfect. Thank you.'

She smiled and turned away, glancing back at him over her shoulder.

'Just as a matter of interest,' she said. 'Seven happens to be my lucky number.'

'Is that a fact? Well, it's always been a favourite of mine. And as we'll be sailing the seven seas, perhaps this is an omen.'

She laughed again. 'Or a curse.'

'I don't believe in curses,' he said, taking off his jacket and making himself comfortable. 'But I do believe that some friendships can last a lifetime. And they say that friends can make the best life partners. And the best poached egg on toast.'

Coming soon

To find out about my next book, and all future releases, please go to: https://www.emilyharvale.com and subscribe to my newsletter via the 'Sign me up' box. Or follow me on social media. There are lots of exciting and wonderfully romantic stories coming soon.

A Note from Emily

Thank you for reading this book. If you loved it and want to be the first to find out about my new books, and also, chat with me and other fans, ask to join the exclusive Emily Harvale's Readers' Club Facebook group. Or go to: www.emilyharvale.com and subscribe to my newsletter via the 'Sign me up' box.

A little piece of my heart goes into all my books and when I send them on their way, I really hope they bring a smile to someone's face. If this book made you smile, or gave you a few pleasant hours of relaxation, I'd be delighted if you'd tell your friends.
I'd also love it if you have a minute or two to post a review. Just a few words will do, and a kind review makes such a difference to my day – to any author's day. Huge thanks to those of you who do so, and for your lovely comments and support on social media.
Thank you.
A writer's life can be lonely at times. Sharing a virtual cup of coffee or a glass of wine, or exchanging a few friendly words on Facebook, Twitter or Instagram is so much fun.

I mentioned my newsletter just now. It's absolutely free, your email address is safe and won't be shared and I won't bombard you, I promise. You can enter competitions and enjoy some giveaways. In addition to that, there's my author page on Facebook and there's also my lovely, Facebook group. You can chat with me and with other fans and get access to my book news, snippets from my daily life, early extracts from my books and lots more besides. Details are on my website but you'll find all my contact links in the Contact section following this.

I'm working on my next book right now. Let's see where my characters take us this time. Hope to chat with you soon. In the meantime, I'm sending you love and virtual hugs. I can't wait to bring you more stories that I hope will capture your heart, mind and imagination, allowing you to escape into a world of romance in some enticingly beautiful settings.

To see details of my other books, please go to the books page on my website, or scan the QR code below to see all my books on Amazon.

Stay in touch with

Emily Harvale

If you want to be one of the first to hear Emily's news,
find out about book releases, see covers, and enter free
competitions, then sign up to her Readers' Club by
visiting:

www.emilyharvale.com

and subscribing to her newsletter via the 'Sign me up'
box. If you love Emily's books and want to chat with
her and other fans, ask to join the exclusive

Emily Harvale's Readers' Club
Facebook group

Or come and say 'Hello' on social media:

 @EmilyHarvaleWriter

 @EmilyHarvale

 @EmilyHarvale

Acknowledgements

My grateful thanks go to the following:

Christina Harkness for her patience and care in editing this book.
My webmaster, David Cleworth who does so much more than website stuff.
My cover design team, JR.
Luke Brabants. Luke is a talented artist and can be found at: www.lukebrabants.com
My wonderful friends for their friendship and love. You know I love you all.
All the fabulous members of my Readers' Club. You help and support me in so many ways and I am truly grateful for your ongoing friendship. I wouldn't be where I am today without you.
My Twitter and Facebook friends, and fans of my Facebook author page. It's great to chat with you. You help to keep me (relatively) sane!

Printed in Great Britain
by Amazon